NEW YORK REVIEW BOOKS
CLASSICS

PEOPLE OF THE CITY

CYPRIAN EKWENSI (1921–2007) was born into an Igbo family in a small city in central Nigeria and raised in the country's rural southwest. He studied Yoruba culture at Ibadan University College before matriculating at the School of Forestry. While working as a forestry officer in 1945, he began writing short stories, which were soon anthologized in both Nigeria and England. In 1951 Ekwensi moved to London on a scholarship to study pharmacy; in 1954 he published his debut novel, *People of the City*. After his return to Nigeria, he worked at the Nigerian Broadcasting Company and married Eunice Anyiwo, with whom he had five children. At the outbreak of civil war in 1966, Ekwensi took a post in the secessionist Biafran government. All the while, he wrote hundreds of short stories and radio and television scripts, as well as dozens of novels, including *Jagua Nana* (1961) and *Burning Grass* (1962), two staples of the Nigerian high-school curriculum. In 1968 he was awarded the Dag Hammarskjöld International Prize in Literature, and in 2006 he became a fellow of the Nigerian Academy of Letters.

EMMANUEL IDUMA is the author of *A Stranger's Pose*, a travelogue, and *The Sound of Things to Come*, a novel. His stories and essays have been published widely. Born and raised in Nigeria, he teaches at the School of Visual Arts in New York, and divides his time between Lagos and New York.

PEOPLE OF THE CITY

CYPRIAN EKWENSI

Introduction by
EMMANUEL IDUMA

NEW YORK REVIEW BOOKS

New York

THIS IS A NEW YORK REVIEW BOOK
PUBLISHED BY THE NEW YORK REVIEW OF BOOKS
435 Hudson Street, New York, NY 10014
www.nyrb.com

Library of Congress Cataloging-in-Publication Data
Names: Ekwensi, Cyprian, author. | Iduma, Emmanuel, writer of introduction. |
Title: People of the city / by Cyprian Ekwensi. ; introduction by Emmanuel
    Iduma ;
Description: New York : New York Review Books, 2020. | Series: New York
    Review Books classics
Identifiers: LCCN 2019039516 (print) | LCCN 2019039517 (ebook) | ISBN
    9781681374291 (paperback) | ISBN 9781681374307 (ebook)
Subjects: LCSH: City and town life—Nigeria—Fiction. | Africa, West—Social
    conditions—20th century—Fiction.
Classification: LCC PR9387.9.E327 P46 2020 (print) | LCC PR9387.9.E327
    (ebook) | DDC 823/.914—dc23
LC record available at https://lccn.loc.gov/2019039516
LC ebook record available at https://lccn.loc.gov/2019039517

ISBN 978-1-68137-429-1
Available as an electronic book; ISBN 978-1-68137-430-7

Printed in the United States of America on acid-free paper.
10 9 8 7 6 5 4 3 2 1

INTRODUCTION

AROUND the time I decided to take writing seriously, my family moved to a new town. Before that, I had spent my school holidays away from home, in houses where the books seemed orphaned and unattended to. I remember filching a worn copy of *People of the City* from a bookshelf, beginning to read it: maybe it could teach me a thing or two about how to write a novel. And since I was only fifteen, I saw no error in lifting entire paragraphs of Cyprian Ekwensi's novel and, after changing the characters' names, putting them into mine. I was anything but subtle. I described a man who, like Ekwensi's Amusa Sango, "was seeing a new city—something with a feeling." And then I continued echoing Ekwensi directly: "The madness communicated itself to him, and in the heat of the moment he forgot his worldly inadequacies and threw himself with fervour into the spirit of the moment." I felt pricked in my conscience, but I figured that my plot was so different from his, and that, being so far apart from him in age and renown, my sin was sure to go unnoticed.

Ekwensi, born in 1921, was one of the first Nigerian writers to publish a novel in English. He was prolific, and by the time of his death in 2007, his output totaled nearly forty novels, along with short-story collections, children's books, and film scripts. *People of the City*, which came out in 1954, predated Chinua Achebe's better-known *Things Fall Apart* by four years and was predated in Britain only by Amos Tutuola's *The Palm-Wine Drinkard*. That no one speaks of Ekwensi as the father of Nigerian literature is perhaps due to the undisguisedly didactic and moralizing character of the stories he told.

The clash between tradition and modernity was the central concern of the writers of Ekwensi's generation; his eyes, by contrast, were firmly fixed on the emerging Nigerian middle class—its angsts and lusts and stereotypes—and his work gained a wide readership. In *Jagua Nana*, for instance, published in 1961 (and which won the Dag Hammarskjöld Prize), the lead character is a sex worker. Outraged by the sexually explicit language in the novel, the Catholic and Anglican churches in Nigeria vehemently disparaged the book, and it was banned in schools. *People of the City* had already introduced the themes and setting he would return to throughout his career: the city as a "hill" of wrongdoing, where "everyone mounts his own and descries that of another."

People of the City is set in the late 1940s to early 1950s, in an unnamed city, at a time when West African countries were clamoring for self-government and independence from Britain. The colonial officers began to relinquish control to indigenous civil servants, politicians, newspaper editors, and detectives. Connections between Nigeria and Britain remained close—Nigerians didn't require visas to travel to Britain. In 1951 Ekwensi won a scholarship to study pharmacy at London University. While on the ship to England, he began work on *People of the City*. The book, written by a young man en route to the center of the British Empire, reflects his impatience with colonial dithering: the people of West Africa now had sufficient wisdom to govern their cities; it is time for the British to go.

Any Nigerian writer who has tried to write about Lagos as a city with feeling descends from Ekwensi. Starting in 2005, with Sefi Atta's *Everything Good Will Come*, the last decades have seen that cohort grow in number. Atta's feminist novel covered 1971 to 1995, years of military dictatorship, a time when it was nearly impossible to keep family life and politics apart. In contrast, Teju Cole's *Every Day Is for the Thief*, set sometime around the mid-2000s, after the country's return to democracy, is the introspective account of a Nigerian who has been abroad coming back to the city where he once lived. And the collection *Lagos Noir*, edited by Chris Abani in 2018, includes thirteen stories that, as Abani writes in his introduction, capture "the essence of noir, the unsettled darkness that continues to lurk in the city's streets, alleys, and waterways."

Amusa Sango's city is surely dark and unsettling. He is a crime reporter for the *West African Sensation*, and he knows, we are told, the "smell of news." In one instance it is the story of a woman and her child killed by men to whom she'd lent her husband's gramophone. In another it is a ritual murder of a man by a society that he'd joined to better his fortunes, and whom they kill after he refuses to turn over his firstborn son. Amusa can sniff out the news because he knows the city he lives in, its drive to get ahead, and the dangers that lie in the way. "What is the secret of getting ahead in the city?" he asks. Later, at his first meeting with Beatrice the Second, the woman he'll eventually marry, he says, "The city is overcrowded, and I'm one of the people overcrowding it. . . . If I had your idea, I would leave the city; but it holds me. I'm only a musician, and a bad one at that. A hack writer, smearing the pages of the *Sensation* with blood and grime."

He realizes, like many city dwellers, that year by year it becomes more difficult to disentangle his idea of fortune from the city's promise, one that may well prove to be illusory or instead bring misfortune. Amusa makes strategic alliances and finds the door shut in his face as a consequence or succumbs to his naïveté: he is evicted from his house after his friend raises an uproar there; when he writes a story favoring that same friend, he finds himself fired.

But Ekwensi also builds Amusa up. Well-known as a crime reporter and the leader of a highlife band—"a most colourful and eligible young bachelor"—most girls in the city have his address. Although he is a catch, he is engaged to be married to Elina, who is in a convent, but from the start of the novel he is pursued by Aina, whom he sleeps with and feels conflicted about but refuses to make happy. His marriage to Beatrice receives the reluctant blessing of her father.

Unemployment, homelessness, women who wear "loose, revealing trifles, clinging to the body curves so intimately that the nipples of the breasts showed through"—Amusa must struggle with all these. That the arc of a man's life tends toward marriage, that his prestige is underscored by the match he makes, is as prominent a theme in the novel as the vagaries of the city. The people of the city are sexual beings, men and women all lusting after one another (even if Ekwensi's women often seem more eagerly lascivious than their male partners).

For twenty-six-year-old Amusa, the story ends with the prospect of happiness. His bride says to him, "Amusa, let's snatch happiness from life *now*—now, when we're both young and need each other." Nothing is said about work and getting back on his feet. What matters is his youth, and the triumph of love.

By 2100, Lagos is estimated to become the largest megacity in the world, with eighty million inhabitants. There is a jostle—in academia, policymaking, speculative fiction, futurist studies—to propose what kind of city it will become. Are there hints to be taken from Ekwensi? If the Lagos that inspired his writing in the late 1940s was already overcrowded and subject to the sorts of clichés that remain current, how about the Lagos of 2100? What the city demands most, as an antidote to failure and prerequisite for survival, is wariness.

When I lived in Lagos, as a teenager with my family and as an adult making a life on my own terms, the size of the place made it cheerless. The scale of desperation unfolding in front of me made me anxious; I had a hunch that many people, including my friends and family, might not realize their dreams of a better life. Yet though many Lagosians pray for a miracle or breakthrough in their businesses, they also rely on something other than the supernatural: they are streetwise; they know an opportunity when they see one.

In Lagos, a story is told about a teenage boy who picks up a stray naira bill, an insubstantial sum, and there and then he turns into a yam. People who saw this transformation gathered around, distressed. They agreed to wait for someone to pick up the yam. A man with a limp showed up, sliced off a chunk, and blood spurted out. Then for several minutes he chanted unintelligible words. Right before the eyes of the agitated crowd, the yam reverted to a boy with a bloodied right ear.

In another version of the story, the teenage boy pisses on the bill before picking it up. He stays human and proceeds on his way, eager to spend the money.

In *People of the City*, the city remains nameless, even though numerous clues—the use of Yoruba in conversations, a rendezvous by the lagoon—point to it being Lagos as where this story of Amusa's coming-of-age takes place: or really an archetypal West African city. The atmosphere is noir, and everywhere vice is interleaved with virtue.

—EMMANUEL IDUMA
Lagos, February 2020

PEOPLE OF THE CITY

Wrong-doing is a hill; everyone mounts his own and descries that of another.
West African Proverb

PART ONE

*How the city attracts all types and how the
the unwary must suffer from ignorance of
its ways*

I

Most girls in the famous West African city (which shall be nameless) knew the address Twenty Molomo Street, for there lived a most colourful and eligible young bachelor, by name Amusa Sango.

In addition to being crime reporter for the *West African Sensation*, Sango in his spare time led a dance band that played the *calypsos* and the *konkomas* in the only way that delighted the hearts of the city women. Husbands who lived near the All Language Club knew with deep irritation how their wives would, on hearing Sango's music, drop their knitting or sewing and wiggle their hips, shoulders and breasts, sighing with the nostalgia of musty nights years ago, when lovers' eyes were warm on their faces. Nights that could now, with a home and family, be no more. While those who as yet had found no man would twist their hips alluringly before admiring eyes, tempting, tantalizing . . . promising much but giving little, basking in the vanity of being desired.

Of women Sango could have had his pick, from the silk-clad ones who wore lipstick in the European manner and smelled of scent in the warm air to the more ample, less sophisticated ones in the big-sleeved velvet blouses that feminized a woman.

Yet Sango's one desire in this city was peace and the desire to forge ahead. No one would believe this, knowing the kind of life he led: that beneath his gay exterior lay a nature serious and determined to carve for itself a place of renown in this city of opportunities.

His mother had seen to it that he became engaged to 'a

decent girl from a good family, that you might not dissipate your youth, but sow the seed when your blood is young and runs hot in your veins . . . that I might have the joy of holding a grandchild in my arms'.

Many of Sango's sober moments were spent in planning how he would distinguish himself in the eyes of his mother, an ailing woman in the Eastern Greens whose health had steadily broken down since Sango's father died two years previously. She was no longer young. Sango did not know how old she was, but he was twenty-six and an only son. Every letter of hers expressed anxiety that Sango had to work so far away from home, and cautioned him about a city to which she had never been.

He had received one of them only yesterday, just before he met another of those girls he had been begged to avoid. And he had fallen. To make up for this lapse and to prove that from now on he really meant to be 'good', Sango had been up since 4.20 a.m., working on the report of an inquest. Now it was nearing 6.30 a.m., and he knew that if he did not wake his servant Sam his morning bath would not be served and he might be late for the office.

The door was slightly ajar and Sango was startled to hear a furtive knock. The room had already darkened and the caller stood behind the half-open door waiting to be invited in, yet too polite to intrude.

'Who's that? Come in, if you're coming in!'

'Are you alone, Amusa?'

A female voice, a female hand, elegant: a girl, ebony black with an eager smile. She smiled not only with her teeth and her eyes, but with the very soul of her youth. She wore one of those big-sleeved blouses which girls of her age were so crazy about. Really, they shouldn't, for the *bubas* were considered 'not good' by the prudes: loose, revealing trifles, clinging to the body curves so intimately that the nipples of the breasts showed through. Certainly not the most comfortable sight to confront a young bachelor on a morning when he had just made noble resolutions. Amusa tried to appear unmoved. Her large imitation-gold ear-rings twinkled in the dim light. She moved across the room gracefully. Sango felt the vitality of the girl and it tantalized him.

She came over to the edge of the table where he was working and rested her hands. This simple movement had the effect of throwing up her bust, so that it swelled within the loose blouse. She smiled.

'Don't you ever rest? Last night you were playing trumpet at the club.'

'Don't remind me about that one; I must get on with my report. By the way, where are you going all dressed up like this?'

'I've come to see you.' The smile had vanished and Aina seemed suddenly aware of herself.

'Very kind of you, Aina; but my mother will not be pleased to hear that I spend my time in this city receiving pretty girls in my room at seven in the morning!'

She looked away. She looked down at her slender, shapely hand. She looked into his face. He saw the tears in the dark eyes and thought: now, now . . . not this morning!

'Come, come, Aina! I didn't mean to speak harshly. You're looking so very pretty this morning. I love your *buba* and the careless ease with which you always dress. Aina, you're a man-killer. Ah, now you smile. But I see a darkness in your face. Tell me, what is it?'

'I – I – No! Let's leave it till another time.'

'Please tell me. Do you want something? Is there a way I can help?'

'No, Amusa. Let's leave it like that. Please fetch me some paper. For wrapping.'

Amusa found her some paper. He was wondering when she would come to the point. She took it from him and went to the corner of the room. He saw her quickly take something from the folds of her cloth and wrap it up. Then the crackling of paper ceased and she came to him once more, smiling.

5

'Thank you, Amusa. I want to ask you something. Amusa, will you always love me as you did yesterday, no matter what happens?'

'Like what? I don't understand.'

'Answer me. Will you always love me?'

'Yesterday?' Sango asked.

To him the past was dead. A man made a promise to a girl yesterday because he was selfish and wanted her *yesterday*. Today was a new day. He had met her at one of those drum parties they always held on Molomo Street. Almost any night you could walk in among the singers and drummers. A marriage, a christening, a death: no matter what it was, the incandescent lamp always shed its rays on the girls who hovered around the glitter like moths. Sometimes the girls danced and then the young men would pinch one another and point to something appealing in a new girl. Sango had been bored with the party until he had seen Aina standing alone, tall and graceful, waiting, he imagined, for the man who could stimulate her imagination.

He had been that man. It had not been easy, for Aina had come to the city and was attracted by the men, yet very suspicious of them. Not even the festive throbbing of the drums could break the restraint which her mother, and the countryside, had instilled in her. But Sango was the city man – fast with women, slick with his fairy-tales, dexterous with eyes and fingers. It had required all his resources, and when they had parted, a little after midnight, Sango had known the intensity of her passion. To be reminded of last night's abandon so early the next morning was like being faced with a balance sheet of one's diminishing prestige.

'Amusa, do you like me still? Do you love me? If anything happens, will you always love me? We are both young, and the world is before us . . . All I want is your word.'

'Is it important?'

He saw the struggle in her eyes. What could this mean? Could there be something else? What did she want of him?

Her fingers were restless. Her firm bosom heaved against the clinging blouse. Again that mad longing to touch her welled up in him.

Suddenly she met his gaze squarely. 'Have you no feeling at all?'

Before he could answer she turned swiftly and was out of the room. He heard the crunch of her retreating crêpe soles on the gravel.

This girl must be treated like the others. She must be forgotten. She must not be allowed to be a bother to him. Every Sunday men met girls they had never seen and might never see again. They took them out and amused them. Sometimes it led to a romance and that was unexpected; but more often it led nowhere. Every little affair was a gay adventure, part of the pattern of life in the city. No sensible person who worked six days a week expected anything else but relaxation from these strange encounters. Aina must know that. Sango had his own life to lead, his name to make as a band-leader and journalist. All else must be subordinated to that. Nothing must be allowed to disturb his plans.

Yet he was disturbed. Now that she had gone and the scent lingered in his room, he wanted her. He went to the door and called: 'Sam!'

Sam came quickly enough, wiping his hands on the seat of his khaki shorts. His red shirt was unbuttoned all the way down the front, revealing the hard muscles of his chest. He could be fifteen or fifty. He had the youthful gaiety of a boy of fifteen and the cunning of a grandfather.

'Is she gone?'

'Who, sah?'

'Come on, Sam! You saw her.'

Sam smiled cunningly. He had that ideal quality of a bachelor's houseboy: a complete and thorough knowledge of the women with whom his master associated. Their names, their addresses, their real cousins and false cousins, their moods. . . . Not only did he know how to deliver a letter to

7

CYPRIAN EKWENSI

a prospective mistress without embarrassing her, but he could also read faces and guess the innermost thoughts of the lady's heart. And these unique qualities covered up his other faults and rescued him from the bane of unemployment.

He scratched his head. 'I am in the kitchen, washing plates. I don't see anyone, sah!'

'I believe you, Sam.'

'I'm sorry, sah.'

'Okay!'

Sam hesitated a moment.

'Coffee or tea, sah?'

'Coffee, and make it black.'

Sam took the percolator from the table in the corner and went out of the room. Sango could hear him asking the two street women who lived next door whether they had seen anyone leave his master's room and pass along the corridor.

Sango sighed. 'Shan't be bothered about her any more. A funny girl. She's the one in dire need of something. But rather than ask for it, she'll bluff and put on a mystery act, expecting *you* to go down on your knees and beg her. And if you don't, then you're hard-hearted. That's life. That's women all over. Yes, I've begged and coaxed . . . when I'm in need. But this morning? No, I must be good.'

He pulled his chair closer to the table and settled down to writing his report:

Popular opinion does not incline favourably towards this verdict of suicide. During the investigations it seemed as if a foregone conclusion had been arrived at. The prosecution tried to prove its theory of suicide. And it appeared as if the learned judge co-operated with them. I ask, what had the judge to fear? Why did he suppress – or gloss over as if in haste – all the evidence which tended to create the faintest suspicion of doubt as to what really happened?

That a gun lay beside the body of the managing director has been firmly established. That it bore his fingerprints is beyond question, and that he was in financial difficulties (as his books show). But do all these necessarily add up to suicide?

The *West African Sensation* can now reveal a phase of Mr. Trobski's private life unknown to the police. Mr. Trobski came to West Africa in the war years when Government was looking for just such a man . . .

He chewed his pencil. Should he throw this bombshell on the city? Yes, in all fairness he must. Too often had murderers been left to go scot-free.

There comes the dreaded city noise, Amusa. You live with it so you don't notice it any more. Sounds of buses, hawkers, locomotives, the grinding of brakes, the clanging of church and school bells. . . . The city was awakening.

When Sango first moved into Twenty Molomo, the faintest noise would bring him racing to the street. And he would get there to find the crowd pressing on the central characters. Once he had seen a husband dragging his wife by her hair because – he had never found out why. All the answers he got were in Yoruba and Sango did not speak the language. Now the scenes had lost their novelty, and whatever he missed he could always pick up at the barber's shop.

The noise grew louder. Something *was* happening. This noise had a hysterical urgency that frightened Sango. Even the cars were checking and now the yelling was rising above the hum of the engines. He decided to remain where he was and finish his report.

He heard the sound of running feet along the corridor. There was a rude and demanding knock.

'*Mr Sango!* Sango, are you in?'

A slippered foot peeped into the room, then a gilt-edged fez cap with golden tassels. Lajide was chewing the end of a cigarette and puckering up his big chocolate-brown face to avoid the fumes getting into his eyes.

'Come here, please.' He beckoned.

How that one-inch of ash remained at the end of his cigarette without dropping off fascinated and annoyed Sango. He got up from his report reluctantly.

'Anything wrong, sir? Haven't I paid my rent? You are

the landlord, but you've never spoken to me so early in the morning. There *must* be something nasty ... anyway I've switched off all lights before going to bed, so it can't be the electricity bill.'

'I just want you to see something for yourself; because of next time.'

Sango regarded Lajide as his one great obstacle in this city, and Lajide in turn often called Sango a vandal, sent by the devil to destroy his property at Twenty Molomo Street. Everything was in order between landlord and tenant except good feeling. Sango took care to make no advances to any one of the extremely attractive harem of eight wives with whom Lajide surrounded himself and flooded his premises.

'Just go up Molomo Street,' Lajide said. 'Go and never mind about your work; you'll come back to finish it.' He squinted through the haze of cigarette-smoke. 'Go, you will see something interesting.' The challenge and the implied insult were intriguing.

Sango was puzzled. 'I'd like to go, but can't you just tell me what it is? It's getting late, and my report —'

Lajide smiled. The cigarette-ash was now one and a half inches long and had not yet fallen off. It had curved slightly. 'Just go up the road . . .' The noise suddenly increased. 'You hear that?' He was jubilant.

Sango did not like unpleasant surprises in the morning before breakfast. From what he could make of it, the voices appeared to be children's. But underlying that was something sensational. Sango could feel it.

'Another husband beating his wife? Are there no police in this city?'

'Is all right, Sango. If you like, you go. You don't like to see your gal frien' naked in de street. When I talk, you say I talk too much —'

'Which gal frien'? Tell me, which gal frien'?'

Sam appeared and said, 'Is true, sah. I tink is the gal who

jus' lef' here. People gather roun' her and laugh at her. Some even slap her, sah!'

On Molomo Street, the traffic was in a jam. Sango made his way through a seething mob of raving lunatics, jeering with excitement. He was quite unprepared for the surprising sight which met his eyes.

A girl was seated on a stone, and for all the world she looked like a model posing for a group of drunken artists who yelled and threw missiles at her. Only, these mad people were no artists. They were people who had wanted her and had not got her. They were revelling in her humiliation. She sat there on the stone paralysed, defenceless and scornfully beautiful. A child came near and with a stick dealt her a blow across the shoulders. She winced. Everyone shouted and booed.

'Thief! Thief! *Ole! Ole!*'

Could this be the same girl in the blue velvet wrapper and the imitation-gold ear-rings? He had suspected that she had something on her mind, but she had been too proud to say just what. Sango pinched himself to make sure he was not dreaming. Aina was seated there on the stone, fully alive to the stone-throwers and the yelling mob. He must do something. It would be foolish to face the mob.

'*Ole! Ole!*' (Thief! Thief!)

'A thief? What has she stolen?'

'She's sitting on it . . . that green cloth.'

'*That one?* But —'

'Yes!'

'But it is worthless.'

'She stole it.'

'Look at her lover! I know him.'

Someone was pointing and Sango knew he had been identified.

'Yes, that is her lover – the lover of a thief-woman. These Lagos gals. When they make up you don' know thief from honest woman.'

'Ha, ha!'

Now Sango understood why Lajide had been so insistent that he should see things for himself. At the other end of the street a policeman was pacing up and down, quite unconcerned. Sango ran towards him.

'Constable—' He tried to catch his breath. The traffic drowned his voice. 'Constable —'

'I'm a corporal,' said the man.

'Oh, sorry. Corporal. Are you going to stand there while they kill the girl?' He pointed down the road at the crowd. 'Please help her quick. Only your uniform can save her.'

'I'm on point duty here. What girl? Not that street girl?'

'This is no time for that, Corporal. Protect her first, then judge her. It's your duty!'

'What did she do?'

'Stole a cloth, they say!'

'You think that if she had husband and family, she would go and steal? Is because she's a street walker. The devil finds work for the idle.'

'Please, now! They're stoning and beating her.'

'Softly, my friend. Why so hot? Or is she your girl, eh? Is she your girl? Tell me why you're so hot!' He waved his arm. The oncoming traffic stopped. He was working and talking at the same time. To Sango it appeared as if they had been talking for hours. The corporal went to a little post near by, opened a metal box, took out a phone.

He turned to Sango. 'Why didn't you ring 999?'

'Because I saw you so near. I just wanted protection for her, that's all.'

'*Hello* . . . Corporal Daifu here . . . Molomo Street . . . Yes, proper street gal . . . They want to kill her with stones. Send patrol van to pick her up quick.' He winked at Sango. 'Over to you. Over.' He hung up, closed the metal box.

'Go now!'

'Thank you.' Even before Amusa Sango could turn round,

the 999 van with the letters POLICE was wheeling into Molomo Street, and the young officers were leaping out while the vehicle was still in motion.

Amusa was pleased.

'I tol' you,' smiled the corporal in triumph. 'But lissen. Man to man, go and warn your gal. Yes, I know she's your gal. You see, person who's not careful, the city will eat him!' He laughed.

The arrival of the van had created a definite sensation. Aina was still there. She was standing now and hugging the gay cloth which she had tied firmly under her armpits, covering her breasts from searching eyes. The young men sighed regretfully. A group of policemen were questioning her, and the crowd, all ears and eyes, pressed against them.

Amusa's arrival created another stir. Elbows dug into ribs. Lips whispered into ears. 'That's the boy friend!'

They parted before him; away from the touch of a man who had loved a thief. Near the policeman, Amusa stopped. Aina looked up from her humiliation and their eyes met. The accusation in her eyes made Sango feel awkward. She seemed to say: 'Didn't you promise you would always love me?' To which question Sango could find no answer in his mind. He heard the policemen questioning her.

'What's the matter? Can't you answer the question?'

Aina was silent. Everyone was silent. The policeman barked out: 'Can't you talk? I said what's the matter?'

An elderly corporal said: 'You girls of nowadays, you're too proud. You won't learn something useful, you won't marry; and you're proud. I'll teach you sense!' He turned abruptly. 'To the station!'

'To the station! Yeh! They are taking her to the station!' yelled the crowd.

Aina scowled as if to intimate that she was prepared to face the worst. They bundled her into the car. The crowd booed and sighed. '*Ole! Ole!*'

A woman said: 'I'm sorry. Such a beautiful girl!'

13

'Listen, the thief is saying something. She's talking. Listen to her!'

'Amusa, come and save me! Come and save me, I beg you. If you love me, come and save me! Don't mind what they're saying . . . Come and save me!'

'No,' Amusa said to himself. 'I can't go. I really can't. I was impulsive. I liked you. We had an affair. Let's forget it, Aina . . .'

He looked round and saw the woman standing near him. Tears were coursing down her face. Amusa looked away. To the left of him he heard sneers, whispers, giggles. It would be silly to listen to them or to take offence. They would only laugh all the more and make a fool of him. These were the men who would give anything to have her. Were they not satisfied with her misery as it was?

At the entrance to Twenty Molomo, a man in a gilt-edged cap with golden tassels was waiting. He seemed to be admiring his floral slippers. When Sango approached he looked up.

'You see now?'

'See what?' Sango mumbled in his irritation.

Lajide's cigarette bobbed up and down as he spoke, but the ash did not drop off.

'The girl . . . didn't I warn you about city women? They're no good. They dress fine, fine, you don't know a thief from an honest one. Just be careful, Mr. Sango. Don't bring more thieves here. I don't want them on my premises. Hear that?'

Sango forced a smile. 'Thank you, Lajide. Aina will not come here any more. That is, if she gets out of this mess.'

Sango went back to his report. He read over what he had written, chewed his pencil, and continued:

> The public must be satisfied that he could have died by no other means than suicide. Otherwise that feeling of unsafety will always lurk in the citizen's mind. After all, it is the citizen who pays the tax that pays the police. Therefore he must be protected from gangsters, hooligans, robbers, rich men who flaunt authority . . .

He looked over the last sentence. There was something

there. The public liked a paper which spoke up. The Trobski murder had something unsavoury about it, and the *West African Sensation* would not let those concerned make a mess of things. People would speak of the *Sensation* as the fearless paper.

2

Sango did not hear the knock but looked up when the doorway darkened. The tall woman who came in could have been fifty or sixty or eighty. Her jowls were shrunken, and a pathetic expression lingered in the depths of her wine-red eyes. She was a total stranger to Sango.

'Take a seat,' he said with reverence. He was afraid.

She sat down very slowly, assessing him. Something in her manner chilled the beating of his heart.

'She sent word to you . . .'

'Who?'

'My daughter, Aina.'

Sango flopped into an arm-chair. He could not see the resemblance between Aina and the old woman. But he felt the slow, confident grip of her power over him. The word 'witch' occurred somewhere in his subconscious, but he quickly dismissed it as out of date. She was behaving with the air of a mother-in-law in the tenth year of her daughter's marriage.

'She said you should come and bail her . . . they want to put her in jail.'

Amusa Sango bit his lip.

'You have been very kind to her so far . . .'

Amusa jerked himself up from his seat. 'Me?'

'She hides *nothing* from me. She is my daughter, and I trained her, since she was like this . . .' She made a motion to show Aina's height at the age of taking the first steps.

How much did this woman really know? What was at the back of her mind? Amusa thought of her age, of the generation in which she had grown up, and he became afraid. *I wish my mother were here to match her magic against your magic, if that's what you're trying to use against me. You know I am young. I may be able to read and write, I may work in a big office, but I am as a child where your worldly wisdom is concerned. I wish my mother were here.*

'So, Aina told you about this place?'

'Yes; and your servant, Sam. He comes from near our village. You know we are not Lagos people. We only come here for a while.'

Your servant Sam. But – no, Sam wouldn't do that. He wouldn't take a powder from you to sprinkle over my breakfast beans. I have been very kind to him. So that's out of the question. You cannot poison me through Sam.

'Well, I'll think about it. I'll see if I can help her.' He tried desperately to sound all-powerful and authoritative. 'But if she has really stolen that cloth —'

'Don't listen to them.' The energy behind her words startled him. She had absolute faith in the honesty of Aina. She rose. 'I want to tell you this: I may leave the city without notice. My work involves travelling to Abeokuta. I sell cloth, you see.'

'The same thing here,' said Amusa. 'It is going to be as if I run away, if I bail her and leave the town. That is against the law.'

She did not understand. Her wine-red eyes were regarding him malevolently. He broke off, his mouth half open. In that moment he felt the full impact of the woman's power. He knew he had no other choice than to obey.

He called at the charge office after breakfast. Aina was not there. A policeman told him that along with other prisoners —

'Prisoners? Magistrates Court No. 2? What are you talking about?'

'Yes. Her case will be tried this morning.'

When Sango got to the magistrate's court, the magistrate had not arrived. A number of men and women sat inside and outside the court, waiting. Some of them had waited six months for their cases to be heard. And yet Aina's case was being heard so very soon.

Sango saw the Black Maria standing under the mango tree. It was empty. Looking upstairs he saw a window with stout iron bars. A dangerous-looking man with a grizzled beard tried to bend the bars. What if he did? Could he survive a fifty-foot fall to the traffic below? Sango looked at the next window and saw only women. An overwhelming flood of shame swept over him. Aina would be with them. But why did he feel ashamed? What was different about her case? He had often come here to this same court and it had meant nothing to him. He went back into the court and sat in the wooden chair and looked at the magistrate. This was Dirisu, a man feared for his cold-blooded strictness. Around the table a handful of police inspectors, plain-clothes detectives of the C.I.D., shuffled papers. They looked important, with that power to grant or remove personal freedom.

The prisoners began to trickle in, but Sango was looking for a particular one. Suddenly there was a hum. Aina was led into the court. Amusa felt a lump rise in his throat. He should have done something to save her, but hadn't. As it was, she stood alone against a city determined to show her no mercy. She would never win. Sango could hardly bear to look at her face, grey and drawn with suffering, the sheepishly straining eyes, one of which appeared to be swollen.

From the witness box she was repeating after the policeman: 'I promise to speak the truth, the whole truth, and nothing but the truth, so help me God.'

It all looked so formal with a constable standing behind her in the witness box. 'On 26 March at 0430 hours you, Aina, did enter and break into the residence of Madam Rabiyatu Foleye of 19A Molomo Street and at the said time did remove, without her prior knowledge or consent, one wearing apparel, valued at £30. Do you plead guilty or not guilty?'

'Guilty!' came the faint voice. This must have been what the young policeman told her the night before. Do not say 'not guilty' because that will complicate things and annoy the magistrate. Plead guilty and he will be lenient. You will be fined, that's all. A few pounds at the most. Her voice came up again. 'I – I stole the cloth. I am guilty.'

'You are guilty?' There was a sneer on the magistrate's face.

'Yes, your worship.'

A moment's silence as heavy as the entire twenty years of Aina's life. What would happen now? Sango wanted to disappear immediately.

'Three months!' The magistrate's voice was like a whiplash. 'Next case!'

And immediately an old woman at the back of the court broke out in a wail. Two policemen seized Aina. She fought violently, kicking their shins, clawing, biting. 'O, my mother! My mother, come and save me. O Lord, I am dead – O!'

But the stalwart men had been hand-picked and she might just as well have saved her breath. 'Ha,' they laughed. 'Your mother did not follow you on *that* day! Ha!'

Amusa sat cowed. His limbs were heavy and inactive, his throat parched. He needed a drink. He got up ponderously; walked out of the court. Under the mango tree, the Black Maria was leaving. He caught a glimpse of the policeman with the rifle at the back door, Aina's slim waving hand through the bars. She still clung to him even when condemned.

An old woman shuffled beside Sango. She stopped, and said: 'Thank you for all you did, and may God bless you.'

He did not need to look at her, could not bear it. He heard her footsteps as she walked up to the mango tree, mumbling in her dejection; and then he was alone.

3

When Sango got to the *Sensation* office, McMaster, editorial adviser, had not yet arrived. Amusa talked to the art sub-editor about the poor quality of the sports pictures that had appeared in recent issues of the paper. He saw the night editor, Mr. Layeni, shuffling towards them with sleepy eyes. Sango looked at him, said good morning, and continued talking to the art sub-ed.

Layeni stopped. He was one of the old school of Africans who believe that the younger generation were getting too cute. They were rude, did not bow to their elders as of old. They called it 'education', but he had another word for it. They lacked 'home-training'. He would show them. He always showed them.

'Why didn't you greet me?' he demanded of the art sub-ed. 'That's how you younger people disregard your seniors. I don't profess to be very educated, but I'm your senior in age.'

'But I said good morning; Sango, did you not hear me?' The art sub-editor stared helplessly round the office. Protesting and apologizing voices were raised from all tables. The art sub-ed was told to say good morning again, which he did, but Layeni continued to harass him at the top of his thin voice. He was now in the position of a man who has started a row for which no one has any use. He was merely talking to keep face. No one listened to him. He had become a nuisance.

All of a sudden his manner changed. He stopped near the

stairs, looking down. Sango followed his gaze. The man coming upstairs wore a gilt-edged velvet fez with golden tassels. He was smoking a cigar, and smoking it as only a big man knows how. His robes radiated wealth.

'That's Lajide coming,' Sango said.

'Perhaps he wants to insert an advert in the *Sensation*.'

Lajide waved his cigar. 'Hello! How is everybody?' His voice was warm and friendly.

Everybody was all right. Everybody waited to know the source of this sudden display of goodwill. Lajide joked. He laughed at the inconvenience of leaving one's home at night to work for somebody. But people had to do it. It was the same in all countries. If people did not work at night, things would not go on. Layeni laughed, but Sango could see that he was nervous about something.

'Well,' Layeni stammered. 'I – I must be going now.' He looked about him, smiling uneasily.

Lajide blocked his way. 'It's you I've come to see. That's why I'm up so early.'

'Me?' said Layeni.

'I've come to collect my money.'

'Ha, Lajide! Give me some more time!'

Lajide's whole manner changed. The warm and friendly smile vanished into the hot morning air. On his face appeared that cold metallic sheen so familiar to financiers. He had become a snake contemplating his hypnotized victim.

'Every day you say give me time, but I don't see a penny. And you are paid every month.'

'I'll pay . . .'

'That's what you always say.'

'End of this month,' Layeni pleaded. He looked quite subdued and sober standing there, his feet arrested and frozen in a movement contrary to the direction he was facing. All the blustering and bullying had faded from him.

In the office, they whispered about him.

'Drinks too much . . .'

'What does he do with his money? He earns a fat salary yet he owes. Everywhere he's in debt! God save us!'

'And we, his juniors, can manage on our poor salaries...'

'But you haven't a wife and children.'

'Children! Does he pay their school fees? Don't you see them coming here every day to ask for fees? I wonder, such a man! And he claims to be old and sensible!'

Lajide said: 'I'm waiting, Layeni.'

'The old drunkard,' someone muttered. 'He doesn't respect himself, and he expects us to respect him.'

The phone rang. Sango went over.

'*West African Sensation.*'

'May I speak to the editor, please?' The voice was strained, excited and high-pitched. Sango could feel the tension.

'Not in the office.'

'Any reporter there?'

'Amusa Sango, crime reporter. Who's speaking, please?'

The office became silent. Even Lajide and his debtor had frozen and were staring at the telephone with expectant mouths. Sango knew the smell of news. It always gave him a kick. The breeze blew in from the windows, scattering the papers. No one tried to pick them up. The telephone voice was louder, more tinny than ever, clear enough to be heard by all in the room.

'If you want something for your paper, come at once to the Magamu Bush, and you'll get it. Never mind who I am.'

'Magamu Bush. Where are you speaking from? Hello, Hello . . . He's gone, hung up! I must get out to the Magamu Bush at once.'

He went across to the map and stared at it. It was an uninhabited part of the city on the road that led from the wharf. Sango had a vision of a broken motor road lined on both sides by dense woods, swamps and bogs. How often had the *Sensation* drawn the attention of the authorities to the need for developing this area! The crimes committed there were becoming tiresome and monotonous.

'Be careful, Sango,' someone said, as he put on his hat at the rakish angle he loved. The typewriters were clattering again, someone was picking up and sorting out the scattered papers. Lajide was saying: 'Attend to me, Layeni. I'm a busy man, you know that!'

He went outside and hailed a *Sensation* van. In half an hour he was at the railway crossing. The gates had just closed in front of him. Sango fumed and got out. It was always like this. The gates always closed when he was in a hurry. A single shunt engine steamed up. It stopped in the middle of the road and rail junction. The driver in his blue jeans wiped his forearms with waste and smiled. He got down and a woman in blue, with a child strapped to her back brought him a tray and he began to extract the plates of food. His fireman leaned out, shovel in hand, and said something.

Sango looked back. The queue of traffic was now a mile long, awaiting the pleasure of the shunt engine driver and his wife (or mistress).

'They killed somebody in the Magamu Bush —'

Sango heard the words distinctly. He was furious with impatience. The shunt engine belched smoke. The driver's wife (or mistress) moved away. She and her child waved at Papa. Papa climbed slowly back and the engine moved away. The gates swung open. Everyone wanted to get through at the same time. Some day the city would learn to build rail and road crossings on different planes as they did in sensible cities. Sango's van was not the last in the queue of cars, vans, trucks, wagons, bicycles, motor-cycles and scooters. Bells were clanging, horns were screeching and blasting, the entire junction had been transformed into a mixture of fire engines and ambulances in a hurry to get to a church and school where all the bells were ringing at the same time.

'Drive fast,' Sango begged, but it was unnecessary. The mad noise was enough command.

Magamu Bush was not difficult to locate. As they neared it, Sango saw the number of cars parked close by. The van parked on the side of the road and Sango stepped into the bush. People who met him had grave and frightened faces. They picked their way with awe. He barged his way through the crowd and arrived at the front of the huge crescent.

She was lying on the floor, dead. They had killed her, and her child too. Must have torn the poor thing from her back in a fury. Evidence of foul play was there on the floor beside her: two rough-looking clubs. The police in cork helmets and white cuffs took measurements, glanced at their watches. They entered figures methodically into their black notebooks while a photographer flashed lights at the bodies.

'Some people are heartless,' someone said. 'I can't understand it. Kill the woman, yes. But the innocent child – no! That's too much!'

'Too bad,' said an old man. 'And she don't do them nothing.' He folded his arms across his brown jumper.

'You mean they killed her for fun?' Sango asked.

'What else!' The old man shot back. 'What is a gramophone that they will kill someone for? Of course they were drunk. But does that mean they should kill her? For her own thing?'

'No,' Sango said. 'But in this world many people die defending "their own thing", whether it is a material thing, or just a belief.' He hurried back to the office and wrote:

I have just witnessed the most gruelling murder since I became crime reporter for the *West African Sensation*. In Magamu Bush, I saw her, a woman of twenty-five, lying with face twisted. And beside her lay her child, condemned in all its innocence by a gang of drunks. I saw also the two brutal clubs with which she had been done to death. The question I must ask the people of the city is this: Why? Why was the young woman killed in this heartless manner? And why the child too? The answer is simple: greed. The men who killed her borrowed a gramophone of hers. When she went to collect it, they would not part with it, but lured her into the Magamu Bush. The young woman, unsuspecting, followed the drunkards. And having defiled her in bacchanalian triumph, they clubbed her to death and strangled the child.

Let me assure these criminals that the whole of the Metropolitan

Police, crime branch, is out in full force, looking for them. Let me assure the people of this city that the *West African Sensation* will give the police every support to bring the criminals to justice and to safeguard the life and property of the law-abiding citizens.

The weeks of investigation that followed only confirmed much of what Sango had written. The woman had been killed by drunken men for a quite trivial reason. The two men arrested were bachelors who lived on the outskirts of the city. They had come to the city from a fishing district in the delta of the Great River. They had known Muri as a girl, and now that she was married and lived in the city they looked at her with the same eyes of their childhood.

Her husband worked for a coastal vessel and was often away from the city. They persuaded her to lend them the gramophone while he was away. But Muri heard he was on his way back, and quickly went to them to return the gramophone lest her husband make trouble.

She found them drinking. One of them, Thomas, persuaded her to come with him to a neighbouring bush – the Magamu Bush. 'That is where the repairer lives,' he told her.

'Repairer?'

'Something went wrong with your gramophone. I gave it to him to repair.'

Muri would not go. 'I left no one in the house. Is only me and the child here, and —'

'Come on! We won't take long.'

A little maid who saw Muri leave her home went to the police after a restless night, waiting for her to return. What had actually happened between Muri and the drunken Thomas in that lonely strip of bush no one would ever know.

Sango did not often sit at his typewriter with satisfaction. As Crime Reporter, he had seen the beginning of many crimes that made the headlines, but never the end. In this case, it was different, and hence his smile: MAGAMU BUSH MURDER SOLVED BY CITY POLICE, ran his headline.

Readers of the *West African Sensation* will recall my scathing remarks in these columns some weeks ago about the way the police handled the murder case of Mr. Trobski. Well, I must now hand it to the police for their brilliant performance in the Magamu Bush murder. The man who perpetrated the atrocity, who defiled the mother, strangled and killed the child, this *devil* has now been apprehended by the police. If only the police in this city were as hardworking as the corporal who handled the case, life and property would be much safer in this city, and in the country as a whole.

He paused and looked up. One of the reporters had just come in, and turning to Amusa Sango, he smiled.

'Mystery calls are not always safe – or true.'

'Mine was,' Sango said.

'I just received one of those mystery calls. A complete hoax. Spent the last six hours roaming the wilds.' He looked it, too. He blew at his open shirt while fanning himself with his reporter's notebook.

Sango smiled and continued with his story.

Sango made a routine call at the pathology laboratory near the hospital. From the pathologist's window he had a clear view into the prison yard. As he came down the steps a note was thrust into his hand by a stranger in warder's uniform. Aina wanted to see him, the note said.

'I take you there,' said the male warder, and Sango followed him. He tried hard to imagine what she would look like, but failed.

In a little separate group from the out-patients stood a number of women in numbered white frocks. They all looked alike. Sango saw the female warder in her austere khaki holding a book and checking her stock of mixtures. Beside her stood a pharmacist.

How had the male warder got hold of Aina's message? Were there love affairs behind the barbed wire between prisoner and captor? Sango stood thinking about Aina's power over men and he could not but hand it to her. From an adjoining store a girl – also in a numbered white uniform – came in carrying a freshly-filled winchester bottle of medicine. Amusa's heart missed a beat.

'Aina!' He almost shouted out the name.

She was quite changed. It was incredible, but she was becoming plumper, more seductive. There was a new and wicked glint to her eye. He steeled himself against the choking sensation in his chest. Her suggestive curves showed even in a uniform designed to reduce feminine charms to the barest minimum. Few women with their hair shaved off could have been exciting as Aina was.

The female warder who had brought them down was standing with the other prisoners in the waiting-room, checking stocks. Sango went over towards her, but before he spoke she fixed him with a hostile look.

'I'm sorry,' she said, in answer to his request. 'You cannot see Aina. It is forbidden. Law-abiding citizens are not allowed to speak to prisoners. You may see her on visiting day, next Sunday.'

Sango had seen the flash of eager joy in Aina's eyes. Her eyes were downcast when she knew Sango could not see her. But between the crime reporter and the girl a smile of understanding had passed. Sango felt the sadness and mystery of the whole episode.

4

All day long and all night long, wherever he went, the thought of Aina obsessed him. It seemed as if, in going to jail, she had left behind her something more distracting than her own presence: the silent accusation that he had deserted her in her moment of need. When the knock sounded on his door, he half expected to see her or her mother and would have been grateful to put aside the article he had been trying to work on so unsuccessfully.

It was Bayo. He had a habit of dropping in on Sango whenever he felt like jazz. Sometimes he came alone, sometimes with his friends in their narrow trousers, pointed shoes and dark sun goggles.

He breezed in now. 'Amusa Sango!'

Sango in a shirt and loin cloth was chewing the end of his pencil and puzzling out an article on 'Sporting Criminals'. He looked up grudgingly.

'Hello, Bayo!'

'Always busy!'

Bayo unbuttoned his coat, displaying his zebra-striped shirt. He fanned his face with a newspaper.

'I've got a dame with me,' he confided. 'She's crazy about jazz. I've told her about your records.'

'Where's she? So few people appreciate real jazz —'

'Don't start lecturing yet. May I go and fetch her? I left her at the street corner. Thought you'd be too busy to have us.'

'Not at all.'

'Shan't be long!' Bayo went out. Sango got up to tidy the

room. His working table was in a hopeless mess. The arm-chairs were untidily set on the lino. He straightened the cushions. There was a knock at the door and they came in.

'Sango, Miss Martins – Dupeh Martins.'

'How're you?'

She smelt sweet. Sango took her soft hand gently in his, looking into the black eyes. She was a girl in that dangerous age which someone has called 'the mad age': the mid teens. Her eyes held nothing but infatuation for Bayo. This was a girl who belonged strictly to the city. Born in the city. A primary education, perhaps the first four years at secondary school; yet she knew all about Western sophistication – make-up, cinema, jazz . . . This was the kind of girl whom Sango knew would be content to walk her shoes thin in the air-conditioned atmosphere of department stores, to hang about all day in the foyer of hotels with not a penny in her handbag, rather than live in the country and marry Papa's choice.

As she sat down, Sango put her age definitely at sixteen. Do not be deceived by those perfectly mature breasts. Girls ripen quickly in the city – the men are so impatient. But why did she put rouge on her naturally blooming cheeks? She was pretty enough without it; and besides, it did not blend.

'Well, what will you have?'

'Beer,' Bayo said. 'Brandy for the girl.'

He rose and shuffled towards the gramophone. Sango went out to give Sam instructions. From the corridor he could hear *Basin Street Blues*. Bayo lost no time. He commented: 'One thing I like about Armstrong – he's very original.'

'Sure,' Sango agreed. 'Some good scat singing there.'

'Listen to that! Listen!' He waved his hand to the music. '*Cau!* That's the part I like best. Terrific!'

The girl smiled. 'It send me – oh!'

Sango said: 'There's plenty more there.'

'We're going to enjoy ourselves.' Bayo lounged in the divan. 'By the way, Amusa, I've got a job with the Medical

Department; an uncle's influence did it for me. The pay is not bad either.'

'Congrats, then! I hope you keep it.'

'Things will soon be all right with me.'

'Yes,' Dupeh added cryptically. 'If you don't keep running after girls. You have let them turn your head!'

'Now, now!'

Sango said: 'I'm now going to play a record made in 1906, and I would like you to compare the original dixie-land style with the modern version.'

He put on a record which began with a noise that made Dupeh's face twist.

'Sango,' Bayo said. 'Do you still play at the All Language Club? What's happened to your band?'

'It's there when I can find the time.'

'When next are you playing?'

'Well, I have an engagement —'

'Turn it off, please,' Dupeh said.

'Why, don't you like it?'

'Play something modern. I'm crazy about modern jazz.'

'I'll find you something. Yes, I have an engagement at the All Language Club; crime reporting for the *Sensation* is not enough. But when I return at night, I'm sometimes so tired that —'

Sam came in with four bottles of beer and a packet of cigarettes. 'Ah use the change to buy biscuit, sah.'

He produced a small parcel loosely tied with green paper. As he fidgeted, five biscuits fell to the floor. They were cabin biscuits.

The girl began to laugh. Bayo joined. Sango could not repress a smile. It was all very embarrassing to Sam. He did not see the joke.

'You expect my visitors to gnaw cabin biscuits?'

Bayo wiped the tears in his merry eyes.

'What's wrong with that, Sango? You eat cabin biscuits, don't you?'

'For myself, yes. For my visitors, no!'

'I'm no stranger,' Bayo said. He glanced at Dupeh.

'I'll eat them,' she said. 'I like them with beer.'

'Shame on you, Sango,' Bayo laughed. 'Your boy Sam is very clever and understands our needs.'

Sam was pleased. 'T'ank you, sir and madam. God bless.' He went out.

'A very good boy,' Dupeh said. 'I like him.'

'I'm lost without him,' Sango confessed.

'He's sweet and honest,' said Dupeh. 'I can see that.'

The beer put them at ease. Dupeh and Bayo began with slow lilting dances, clinging together like drowning people. Sango saw that he had become one too many and went back to his typewriter. There were three words at the top of the paper. 'Sports and Crime'. He thought it over, and began to write.

There comes a time when – in contemplating any crime, especially the large-scale, carefully planned type – one has to sit back and muse over the question 'Isn't there an element of sport in all this?'

This thought has come to me because the truly great crime loses its sense of sin and becomes nothing more than a matching of wits – in all fields of human knowledge including super-science – between the law on one side, and the outlaw and socially unacceptable on the other side. The fact still remains that there *is* as much thrill in pursuing a criminal across winding roads, in making one move ahead of him, as there is in watching a football match or a motor race. One difference, though: in a football match the stakes involved are far less gruesome . . .

He glanced up and saw the faith in Dupeh's eyes. Dupeh obviously believed implicitly in Bayo. She must fancy herself in love with him. A girl of that age would believe in the first attractive liar who spoke love to her: therein lay the danger for all unguided teenagers.

Just at that moment Bayo paused, opened his zebra-striped shirt, and blew into it. 'My it's hot! Sango, I wanted to ask you: what about that girl?'

'Who?'

'The one who stole a cloth that Sunday morning?'

'You mean Aina? Haven't you heard? She's in the white college now.'

'Tell me!'

'Serving three months' hard labour. I saw her about five days ago. They had gone to collect medicines at the hospital. D'you know, I wasn't allowed to speak to her?'

'So sorry.' Bayo became suddenly serious. 'Sango, what are your plans about Aina?'

'What d'you mean?'

'I mean . . . but can't you appreciate love? The girl is crazy about you.'

'Well, I'm not crazy about her!'

'You were telling me last time that many women do worse things than Aina, but are never caught —'

'Yes —'

'Is it because she's a —'

'It's not because of anything. I just can't think of marrying her.'

Bayo smiled. 'If I were you, since she has sacrificed so much . . . I mean . . .'

Dupeh cut in: 'Sango, have you got that new record . . . forgotten what it's called . . . er *Kiss me before I fall asleep and dream of you* . . . something like that.'

'That's what we were just discussing, Dupeh. I'm not all that romantic. I only collect jazz.'

'You're out of date.'

'Didn't I tell you,' Bayo smiled.

Dupeh came over and linked her hands with Bayo's. She caressed him, spoke to him tenderly. Sango saw that his presence had become unwanted.

'You've bothered me so much about Aina,' he said. 'Now I'm going to visit her mother. I want to see how she's taking it.'

Sango took his hat and went into the street. He called at Aina's but was told to come back in the evening.

·   ·   ·   ·   ·

Sango was to play at the All Language Club that evening. Towards eight in the evening First Trumpet arrived. While he sat reading a music magazine, Sango changed into the band's uniform: draped flannel coat, black trousers and black shoes. The green ribbon in his buttonhole distinguished him as bandleader.

'Look, Trumpet! I must go out. Just down the road. When the others come tell them I shan't be long. In any case we're not playing until nine.'

First Trumpet winked knowingly.

'Don't be funny. I'm not going to see a girl.'

He walked down Molomo Street. At night the street had a rare mysterious quality that never failed to excite him. Veiled women slipping from hazy light into the intense darkness of the corners; young girls leaving their buckets at the public water-pumps and stealing away under the trees where the glow of a cigarette-end told of a waiting lover and the head-lamps of a passing car would suddenly reveal embracing couples. 'Put out your lights!' the screams and curses would come. 'Put out your lights, you clot!'

Sango stood near the public pump for a moment. He watched the traffic; crossed the road. A few minutes' walk brought him to the house where Aina's mother lived.

It had looked drab enough in the sun, but now the darkness gave it a quality of musty poverty. The only light came from a street lamp some fifty yards away, though the two houses that flanked it fairly glittered with their own lights. On both sides of the main entrance, groups of old women sat, indistinguishable in the gloom. One of them was selling petty things in a wooden cage. On the cage was a hurricane lantern.

'Good evening,' Sango said. He felt on the brink of an important discovery. 'I've come to see Aina's mother.'

'Go in!'

He could not see his way forward. With hands outstretched he groped towards what might be a door. His head caught against something and he ducked. He was in. He could feel

CYPRIAN EKWENSI

that the room was large, like a low-ceilinged hall. In one corner a light flickered. A dark figure approached behind the light. The figure entered a side room. The light faded.

'Welcome,' said a voice, and Sango was startled. 'Welcome again . . . You asked for Aina's mother? I'm here. Move towards this corner. Watch your step!'

He tried to move, but something caught his step and he staggered. Then he realized that the entire floor was covered with sleeping bodies. He was in a kind of bedless open dormitory. Everyone but the old woman slept on the floor. Old, young, lovers, enemies, fathers, mothers, they all shared this hall. From early childhood Aina had listened to talks about sex, seen bitter quarrels, heard and perhaps seen adults bare their passions shamelessly like animals . . . From early childhood she had learnt the facts of life without being taught.

The old woman said, 'Have you seen her?'

'Er, yes.'

'The time is passing . . . Twenty years is not for ever.'

'So you're counting the days?'

'What else is there for me to do?'

'Yes, she'll soon be out all right.'

The old woman coughed. 'Aina had bad luck, too much. People always dislike her, for no reason.'

'You still believe she did not steal the cloth?'

'You're a small boy . . . You know book, you work in a big office, but you are a small boy. You do not know yet the blackness that lies in men's hearts. Such a one as Aina who is young and lively and beautiful. Some wish her nothing but evil.'

Sango was silent. The voice from the dark bed went on: 'One day, I'll tell you what happened, the real truth. But not now.'

Sango asked himself: why did I come here at all? Morbid curiosity, that's all. And now this woman is bluffing. She is going to try blackmail next.

A bicycle grated against a wall outside. A man stood

34

silhouetted against the door. Sango could make out nothing but a heavy dress, and around his shoulders what looked like a thick rope, looped, for climbing palm trees. The man brought into the room a strong smell of alcohol. He marched past Sango and disappeared into the gloom. Sango concluded that he was a wine-tapper back from his work.

The old woman resumed her insistent demands. 'What have you brought for your old woman? You know Aina is gone and now —' She checked herself. 'I am living in hunger. No one to support me.' When he did not respond she went on.

'Aina was working for those Lebanese cloth merchants. She used to give me money every month when they paid her. Now she is in jail, no one gives me money. I am old.'

Sango felt the remark was an accusation. He thrust his hand into his coat pocket and brought out a wad of notes. It was the band's money, and goodness knew from where he hoped to replace it. He tossed the notes on the bed and got out fast.

5

By ten o'clock the All Language Club was full, and still more people came. They liked what the Club was trying to do. No bars – social, colour, political, or religious. There were two bars, though; a snack bar, and one plentifully supplied with all percentages of alcohol right up to a hundred.

Some people came because they liked Sango's music, or the music of the Hot Cats Rhythm, or the Highlife drumming of the unsophisticated Nigerian bands. They came in couples, they came alone and unescorted and sat under the palm trees and smoked and watched the bright lights.

Sango in his spotless jacket announced the next number. He winked at one or two girls. They winked back and trailed on after their wealthy and influential escorts.

Sango's trumpet caressed his lips. The notes came tumbling out, slickly, smoothly, with all the polish of a Harry James; yet sometimes they were clear, high and tremulous with passion as if this young city lad were modelling his style after Louis Armstrong. Nobody noticed; nobody bothered. In the middle of a clever solo, Sango noticed Bayo and Dupeh enter the Club. They were selecting a table while a waiter hovered around them.

Yet more people came. Towards the small hours they poured in from the cinemas, from the other clubs with early-closing licences. A very short man was trotting beside a girl who might have come from the pages of a South Sea travel book. Yet Sango knew she was a West African. Everything about her was *petite*, delicate. Her almost transparent dress was cleverly gathered at the waist. Her ear-rings and smile shone.

'Who is she?' Sango asked, with a heart now beating faster. His eyes followed her to her seat.

'I don't know,' said the First Sax. 'My, my!'

'Who is she?'

Faces lifted from music scores. Heads shook. 'Don't know her . . . Must be new! Yes, sir!'

Sango was conscious of that strange excitement which had possessed him that night when he first saw Aina. The symptoms were the same: an insistent restlessness, a desire to be near this creature, to bask in the radiance of her beauty. He could restrain himself no longer, and during the interval went over to Bayo. Behind the dum palm, Bayo was making a scene. He was a little drunk, and Dupeh was having the worst of it.

'I've told you I don't want to be interfered with! If you love me, love my ways! That's my policy.'

Sango stood for a moment, surveying the scene with amusement. Bayo, talking of policy! His sports shirt open at the neck, he was pacing up and down before the table, bellowing and waving his arms. Dupeh sat still, her head drooping. A handkerchief was pressed against her nose. She was crying. A number of men were trying to tell Bayo not to hurt the girl.

'Bayo, come here!' And when he came, Sango spoke in low tones. 'Stop this wretched show you're making of yourself. There's something you must do for me. Look! That girl over there . . .' He indicated her without moving his arm.

'Pale blue dress, sort of off-the-shoulder?'

'Gipsy ear-rings too . . . they're always in the fashion, aren't they? Which reminds me. I have an ear-ring to return to Dupeh! And the condition you left my room in! Sam will never forgive you!'

'Forgive me, Sango; I'll explain. Now what about the **girl**? Champagne on her table! He must be somebody, then!'

'Find out who they are. Okay?'

'Trust me. Got a match?'

Sango walked between the tables back to his band and struck the cymbals. The band boys began to return from various parts of the club. In a few minutes, Bayo came across.

'Her name is Beatrice; the man is called Kofi something or other: a timber-dealer from the Gold Coast. He also runs an over-land transport to Accra.'

He paused, pulling at his cigarette.

'You're fast, Bayo.'

'Was that all you wanted to know?'

'What is she in this city?'

'I don't know what she does . . . she's new. I've never seen her before. They say her mother is here, but I don't know. She's hot stuff, Sango. Keep clear. The Europeans are crazy about her. I hear tales of disputes settled out of court on her behalf. If you're looking for trouble, well . . . remember Aina!'

'I'm not falling for Beatrice, make no mistake. But she looks so much like my fiancée back home in the Eastern Greens. She attracts me.'

Bayo tapped him on the shoulder. He went back to the little table under the palm tree and took Dupeh's hand. Sango was pleased to see them dancing happily together.

But Sango was not being honest with himself. The fleeting picture of Beatrice was giving him no respite. He saw her when he went to sleep. She was with him in his dreams, his waking hours, his band practice. And night after night, Amusa came to the Club. He wanted to meet Beatrice again. He wanted it so badly, he even took to playing for the Hot Cats Rhythm. When he was too early, he passed his time playing darts, or ping-pong, or talking to the barman.

The proprietor had been in the Civil Service when the idea of the All Language Club occurred to him. He wanted to take a practical step towards world unity, he said. To create a place where men and women of all languages and social classes could meet and get to know one another more intimately. It was his earnest desire that the spirit of fellowship created here would take root and expand.

'But as you can see, one cannot do very much without adequate funds.' He smiled. 'Still, we are trying.'

Beatrice came there one night – but not alone. The Englishman who came beside her was a well-known engineer named Grunnings. He lived on Rokiya Hill, a wooded area outside the city. Sango learnt that Beatrice was married to Grunnings – according to African law and custom.

'She has three children for Grunnings,' the barman told him. 'They all go to St Paul's School.'

Sango said. 'When he completes his usual eighteen months tour, does he take her to England with him?'

'No; she goes to her home in the Eastern Greens. Grunnings has just returned from leave in England, as a matter of fact. She has been waiting for him. He's a bit late this time.'

In well-cut evening dress, with his hair well brilliantined, Grunnings was examining the menu and smiling at Beatrice. Grunnings looked fit and attractively tanned. He was about thirty-eight, of medium build, and his smile was friendly. Beatrice was smiling back with an eagerness that made Sango jealous.

He felt sad. 'To think I've spent all my time dreaming in vain!'

Never once did her eyes leave Grunning's face. If only she could dote on me like that, Sango thought bitterly. But it brought him no comfort. What could they have to talk about at such length? Was her life really complete and full? Had she, in marrying Grunnings, a man with a wife and children in England, realized her purpose?

Sango went to the bar to console himself. He climbed on to a stool. Various resolutions were forming in his mind: *I should never come here again; I must forget her – completely.* He must have been there a long time when he noticed her sitting at the other end of the counter. She had a straw between her lips and was sucking an ice-shake.

Her bare arms lay on the counter, while one leg dangled above the chrome-plated rungs. It would be wrong to speak to her, because he did not know her. Even as the thought flashed through his mind her eyes were on his, dancing with a joyful light; and she was smiling. His heart warmed and he was encouraged.

'My husband knows I like this place,' she said. 'He always lets me sit at the bar and suck a cold drink – by myself. You are not playing today?'

'We play when we're engaged.'

'I enjoy your music; I've always wanted to see you more closely . . . My husband has just returned from England, and is very busy. I wish he would bring me here more: I like night life.'

Sango said: 'An engineer who works all day would like to sit with his wife and family; not go hunting bright lights.'

She sighed. 'Grunnings has changed. Whenever he comes back from leave it is always like that. But this time, I shall do something about it.'

She was talking half to herself, half to him; more like someone thinking aloud. Sango had little time to ask himself: why is she telling me all this? Her manner was so engaging. Add to it the fact that a beauty to whom he had attached so much importance should prove human, with her own worries, and the whole dazzling incident became numbing to his reason.

'He's a nice fellow; he loves me very much. But lots of men also love me and I'm going to leave Grunnings . . . Sango, do you know where I can find a room? I want to move from Rokiya Hill.'

'A room?'

'The place is a grave; too quiet and lonely. I like noise; it is not so boring as silence. And I like high life and drinks and music.'

'Let me think . . . My landlord might be able to help you – a man called Lajide. He's a housing agent and lives at Twenty Molomo.'

She raised an eyebrow and smiled. 'Housing agent! I have no money.'

'Your beauty will see you through, Beatrice. Lajide is a man who likes beautiful women. He has eight wives, but they're not enough. And it will save you wasting a lot of time looking around. In any case, you can always move if you are not satisfied with his offer.'

'You are very kind, Mr. Sango. When I live on my own, I'll be happy. I came here to live and enjoy life. For a short while I enjoyed my life, went to big functions, night clubs . . . I always wanted to be free. Then I met Grunnings and he married me. You will not believe it when I say that he was surprised to find me a complete girl who had known no man before him.'

Sango started. He looked more closely at her. Her eyes were a little too bright, but her voice was low and steady. It was just possible that the champagne, the bright lights, the heady wine and lilting music had affected her a little.

'But now, I have given him three children and I know he can never be a real husband to me, so I'm quitting. I have thought over it a long time!'

She slipped to her feet, smoothly, delicately. No one would ever give this young woman up lightly. She left him and the astounded barman and walked back to her table. Sango could never tire of watching her walk. In his mouth was that sharp taste peculiar to an awakened but unsatisfied craving. At last he had met Beatrice and spoken to her. But what impression had he made on her? He watched her stop at a table. All eyes were on her glittering pearls. Her right arm flashed as she lifted her fingers and placed them gracefully on her forehead. It did not occur to Sango then that something unusual was about to happen.

In the next few minutes the All Language Club was disrupted by one of those dramas which take place so often and are so easily forgotten. Beatrice tried to move on. She couldn't.

She began to sink to her knees. As she fell, Sango bounded towards her.

But Grunnings was there before anyone else and had taken her hand tenderly.

'You're not getting your attack again, Beatrice?' He peered critically into her face. 'I'll take you home.'

'I – I just felt giddy . . . I'm all right.'

She seemed to have shrunken of a sudden. Her hair looked sodden. The lipstick had caked on her lips and her smile was wooden. Never had Sango seen such a rapid transformation. She put her arm round Grunnings's shoulder. Grunnings led her to their seat, collected her handbag and helped her out of the Club.

A waiter ran after them with a bill. Sango stood rooted, perplexed. Could there be so much unhappiness wrapped up in a single person? The waiter joined him, still waving the unsettled bill.

'That woman, one day she will die – like this!' He snapped his fingers. 'She get some bad sick inside her. When them tell her, go home, she no go. One day she go die for this city.'

How true that prophecy proved to be! And how saddened Sango was to dwell on the enigma that was Beatrice. There seemed to be little more to do at the club that night, or perhaps morning. For already it was 2 a.m. Walking home through the streets of the city, Sango met his First Trumpet who had gone to play at an exclusive club on the island.

They fell into step, as both of them lived on the same side of the city. On Molomo Street Sango suggested a late cup of coffee and First Trumpet thought it a good idea. The whole of Twenty Molomo was unaccountably gloomy. It almost reminded Sango of the dingy courtyard in which Aina's mother lived.

'Careful, First Trumpet. We're early sleepers here.'

He led the way. In the corridor, Sam crawled out of his bed, got the keys from his master and helped him open the door. He had that rare quality of continuing to behave like a wide-awake person even though he was fast asleep on his feet.

'There's no light, sah.'

Sango tried the switch himself, in vain. He went out and surveyed the adjacent houses on Molomo Street. Lights were burning gaily in them. It couldn't be a breakdown, then.

'Lajide has started his meanness.'

'It is annoying,' said First Trumpet. 'And we've been out all night. To get home now, hungry and in the dark: what kind of economy is that?'

Sango found a brush and with the pole end began to bang on the ceiling above him.

'Light please!' The idea of Lajide, comfortable and happy with eight women around him rankled in his brain. 'Put on the light, I've paid my rent!'

'He must be out,' said First Trumpet, after a moment's silence.

'Somebody must be in. Lajide, please put on the light; I beg you, put on the light!' The sound of his own voice, ignored, angered him the more.

Sango peered into the darkness and saw a man standing there. 'You have no light too?'

'Yes, I've just come back from the Club. I've been out all evening so no one can accuse me of having wasted current!'

'I have no light, too. I'm the engine-driver living at the other end. I've never seen you, I'm always away on line, but I knew when you moved in.'

Sango could now see the dim outline of the man's heavy overalls and the cap which showed a peak when he turned his face sideways,

'How do you do?' Sango said, shaking his hand. 'An odd meeting, eh?'

First Trumpet said: 'The electricity undertakings have increased their fees by thirty-three per cent. Perhaps that's why you have no light.'

'And the landlords have increased their rent by three hundred per cent, so it balances – with plenty to spare.'

Just then it started to rain. At first one could neglect the drizzle, and then it intensified, pouring with all the vengeance of a tropical tornado.

The woman Rose, who lived next door, produced a hurricane lantern. There was nothing for it but to accept her kind offer and light himself into his room. It was the first time Sango had ever spoken to the prostitute. Now everyone in Molomo Street was awake. At the far end of the passage, the engine-driver was cursing in a venomous stream. Rose came into Sango's room, giggling. She was enjoying the situation immensely. Sango thanked her for her lantern and as soon as she left he and First Trumpet were again plunged into darkness.

'It is not many hours to breakfast,' Sango said. 'You'll have to sleep here, First Trumpet. I want to talk about Beatrice, to pass the time. If you go home now, you will have to wake *your* landlord who may have locked the gate against thieves —'

'I'll stay here,' said First Trumpet. 'But I must be away first thing in the morning. I've got to go to work.'

'Take the bed, then. I'll make myself comfortable on the sofa. And please don't argue with me. I'm dead tired and disappointed with life as a whole.'

'Good night, Sango.'

'Good night, Trumpet.'

Sango awoke. The door was open and the sunlight was streaming in. First Trumpet was gone. On the floor at Sango's feet was a note addressed to him in a feminine hand. Sango picked it up.

He read the copy-book script, no doubt written by a girl – Lajide's lady clerk:

With respect to your attitude last night, it is, and always ever will be, an outstanding rule, that lights should be switched off by 6 every morning, and on the dullest days 6.30 a.m. I am still having 22 points of light and when all the lights are operating I have more dues to pay.

Had I not the utmost patience, you are sure you provoked me to the last yesterday. I have been waiting to receive from you a notice to quit.

But now I must give you one month's notice from this date.

Over his breakfast, Sango tried once again to make sense out of the involved memo. One thing was clear. He had been given notice to quit. This could be more than serious. A man thrown out of his lodgings in the city could be rich meat for the ruthless exploiters: the housing agents and financiers, the pimps and liars who accepted money under false pretences. This matter needed very careful thinking out. If only his nerves had not been in that awful state last night.

Before he had lowered his third cup of coffee, the engine-driver stood at the door. He was in his blue overalls and a blue cap.

'Going to work?' Sango asked.

'Yes . . . Look at this.'

'Oh,' said Sango. 'You got one, too!'

Sango took the note and read:

I, A. O. Lajide, your landlord, do hereby give you notice to quit and deliver up possession of the room with the premises and appurtenances situated and being to No. 20 Molomo Street, which you hold of me as tenant hereof, one month from the service of this notice. . . .

Written in the same feminine hand, it was signed with the same bold scrawl.

'Lajide has not been hanging round the courts for nothing.' He handed over the note, rubbed his head reflectively. 'This is really serious, you know. Where have I the time to search for new lodgings?'

'It's not easy,' said the engine-driver. 'I'm going on line now; I return next tomorrow.'

Sango said, 'Now we shall see how overcrowded the city

really is, with the trains bringing in more and more people every day.'

'I'm not going to sleep in the gutter,' the engine-driver said with confidence. 'New houses are being built every day.'

'For you?' Sango sneered. 'The owners want money, my friend! How much can you pay? A European is able to offer five thousand pounds cash to a landlord, and he gets a tenancy for five years. He takes a whole courtyard that can house one hundred Africans . . . and we are driven to slums like Twenty Molomo.'

The engine-driver said: 'But the Africans are the brothers of the landlords. They can't do that, surely!'

'Brotherhood ends where money begins.'

'I'm going to find a room, all the same.'

'Best of luck! And if you have one to spare, think of me.'

He marched down the corridor in his heavy boots and Sam came in to clear the table. His back was expressive as usual, and he was most sympathetic. He would tell his brother and all the others, but would Master consider going to beg Lajide? He might yet change his mind and that would save a lot of trouble.

Sango smiled. 'Not me, Sam!'

Almost everybody on Molomo Street had heard of the engine-driver's behaviour of the previous night. They came to see Sango and to sympathize with him. Once it was generally known that he did not send them back, yet more of them came. There was the woman who sold rice to the loco workers. Sango had often seen her sitting under the almond tree. He was surprised to find that she could be quite smart when she got out of her oily working clothes. Then there were the two sisters who lived down Molomo Street. The baby-faced one was appealing in a maternal way with folds of fat everywhere and a face that was sweet and peaceful. Sango, as more and more of them knocked and told him they were sorry he was leaving, said to himself: 'I never knew I was the darling of

Molomo Street! How the people love me – especially the women.'

He lay on his back in the night, unable to sleep. This was his usual time for work, when the city traffic had thinned down to a mere trickle and comparative silence descended on Molomo Street; but on this particular evening he did not feel like work. He rolled over and over, gazing at the ceiling. When he heard the knock, it was so faint he could not be sure. But it came again, a mere brushing of the hands against the woodwork. The lines of a poem he had composed flitted through his mind:

> You who knock so secretly
> Sidling up the door, your eyes in veils
> Your feet on pads of silence
> Your manner furtive
> Your breath held in suspense
> Who might you be?
> A thief – that fears to waken
> A household fast asleep?
> And when 'tis asked who knocks
> Why slide you mutely out of sight
> Waiting in concealment
> Hearkening for the voice of whom you seek?
>
> Perhaps you know he knows your knock
> And would not raise a voice
> For fear your call would scandalize the moral world
> So patiently you wait
> And hearing steps that only you can hear
> Your eyes light up with love
> As he with stealth transcending yours
> Slides back the bolt and in his arms
> Takes your sweetly scented arm
> And savours more the fruit that, forbidden,
> Delights the more . . .

He lingered with pleasure on the lines, saying again the more delightful ones: *Your feet on pads of silence* . . . But now the knock had become persistent. He groaned and got out

47

of bed. When he opened the door, he drew back in surprise. A girl was standing there, nestling against the wall.

She could not be more than fourteen, but her breasts were taut and large with ripeness. She had sleepy eyes, a husky voice and soft lips. Sango had often seen her hawking lobsters, a Molomo Street delicacy. Her deep croaky voice set his blood afire.

'Doctor . . . Doctor . . .' He was not a doctor, and only the devil's temptress could tell him where she had got the idea, but it pleased him. He looked up and down the corridor and saw that no one was in sight. This was temptation. She pushed her breasts against the door.

Sango kept the tremor out of his voice.

'What is it?'

'Doctor,' she breathed, and cleared her throat. She made eyes at him. 'Doctor, I heard you are going . . .' Her bare smooth shoulders and rounded arms invited his fingers. He held back.

'Now, girl, go to bed. Quick. All girls of your age are lying in their mother's beds.'

He shut the door. 'Phew!'

> You who knock so secretly
> Sidling up the door, your eyes in veils
> Your feet on pads of silence . . .

He listened. She was still there. He could hear her moaning to be let in. He went to sleep still hearing her calling croakily, 'Doctor . . .' and brushing her hands against the door, 'I want to tell you something. . . .'

6

That afternoon Sango began to search for new lodgings. He found little luck. After cycling miles and miles, he met Dele on the crest of a hill. He had not seen Dele since college days and now he found him virtually unchanged, carrying a Bible, smiling and shy.

'Dele, I'm looking for a room,' Sango told him when they had overcome their mutual surprise.

'A room? Now let me see . . .' He stroked his chin and looked thoughtful. 'Would you like to live in this area?'

Sango looked around him, and saw the logs floating on the lagoon. Logs that would soon be loaded into cargo boats and sent on their journeys to Europe and America. Logs that trapped the still waters and made a happy breeding ground for mosquitoes and malaria.

'I'm looking for a room, Dele, not an area!'

'Then come along! I'm just back from the office. But we may be lucky enough to meet the man I want.'

Sango followed him and learnt that, as the time for the Town Council elections was very near, candidates were willing to consider any proposals that might win them votes. As it happened, the man they were going to see was an election candidate and might help them. He was also an intimate friend of his father's. Dele pushed his bicycle and talked of old days.

So wrapped up were they in comparing notes that Dele overshot his mark and they had to wheel back to find the right door. Dele knocked. While they waited Sango had a glimpse of an expensive cap not unlike Lajide's. But the man who wore it was much darker, stouter and more pleasantly disposed.

'Dele, is that you? Ha, ha! Come in!'

Sango's heart warmed towards the man. He was at a table littered with small cards, labels, posters, pamphlets. Sango could read the inscription on some of them:

YOUR CANDIDATE FOR 'A' WARD IS ... VOTE FOR HIM: WE WILL DELIVER THE GOODS ... OUR POLITICAL MANIFESTO ... AFRICANIZATION OF THE CIVIL SERVICE ... SELF-GOVERN-MENT NOW ... AWAY WITH EXPATRIATES

The words seemed to shout frantically from the very pages. On a large poster was a photograph of the candidate himself, looking dignified in his robes.

Dele said, 'This is my friend, Amusa Sango. We were at school together, after which he went to teach for some time; now he is a journalist.'

'How are you, Mr. Sango?'

They shook hands. It was a warm, confident hand, Sango thought. Dele smiled.

'Yes, sir, as I was saying, he's a journalist. I would like you to help him. Maybe he can write something good about you in the *West African Sensation*. You see, sir, he's looking for a room. As a man who reads a lot, he would like a place that is not noisy; that's why I have brought him to you. Because I know you can help him.'

Sango admired Dele's acting. In his loose but well-cut English suit, he looked boyish. He spread his palms upwards, rolled his eyes, bent his head this way and that in an appealing manner. His gestures were expressive. One would think that Sango was not the one in need but Dele himself.

He paused now, his eyes focused on the election picture. To Sango he said: 'He's the candidate for your ward. The elections are coming on. He's very busy as you can see.'

'Yes,' said the Councillor, beaming. 'I pray I get in. My party fights for the people, for the poor. There are poor men in every tribe and race, therefore my party is the Universal Party. But my rivals!' Here he snorted. 'They're out to line their own pockets! They're out to capture all the highest posts. We must defeat them and have things our own way – for the people's good.'

'I think you'll get in, all right, sir!'

'It's not so easy: the candidate for the other party is not sleeping. He says he stands for the workers – the liar! He tells them I am deceiving them, that I am an aristo. And he gives them money, so they believe him – that's the worst of it! They do not know they are selling their freedom, their birthright, everything decent in them! Oh!'

'He will not get in,' Dele assured him. 'We are voting for people, not parties. The British have given us a new constitution. It is for us to select the best *men* to work it. That is our first and last step towards self-government. You have done a lot for this area. Look at Grave Street. Two years ago, it was all swamp. Not a light anywhere. Now we have water, electricity . . .'

'Oh yes! but when people pass along Grave Street, they don't bother to think. Still, one does not have to wait for thanks. That's a politician's lot. Do the right and leave it at that; that's my motto. And it gets things done.'

He rubbed his chin and beamed. He was pleased. His work was appreciated by the two young men. Sango thought guiltily of his assignment for the *West African Sensation*. But the politician would not come straight to the point.

'I remember when I was a teacher some years ago, things were quite different.'

'Quite so, sir.'

'No African Education Officers, Principals . . . where would you find them? But now things are different. Yes, things are gradually passing into African hands. Soon all the power will be in our hands. It's worth fighting for.'

'You love politics, I can see that,' Sango said.

'Politics is life. Look at it now. After these elections, life will be different. With every election things change. And so it will go on changing, all the time, and one day we'll get what we're fighting for: complete autonomy!'

'Things can't be the same,' Dele said.

'And that's politics. We want our own Government. They will decide what money you may have, what food you may eat; what hours you may sleep; what films you may see: all this is life. Politics is life. I like it.'

'Politics is not for young men like ourselves. For you, it's good. You worked for years under the British Government. Now you have retired. You have your pension. Your children are at the University. What more? You have nothing to risk. But we young men, we are only just starting our lives.'

The Councillor sighed. 'Too much guts. That is the trouble with young politicians. They see one cause, one belief, and they stake their whole life on it, regardless of consequences. An older man tempers belief with tact – that's why he gets through.'

The liberation of his ideas had brought a new and more promising light to his eyes.

'Dele, you know my son.'

'Yes, sir.'

'Well, he returns to the University in October. That's in a few weeks time. He's occupying a room here. Why doesn't your friend share the room with him till he leaves, and then he can have the room to himself. And I don't want any rent from him. If he's in difficulty about meals, my wife is there to help.'

Sango was overwhelmed by the kindness of the Councillor; but knowing his own irregular hours, he did not see how he could live as part of a family. He was silent enough to compose his thoughts.

'I don't know how to begin,' he said and glanced at Dele.

'You're going to accept, of course! The Councillor has been very generous.'

'Thank you,' said the Councillor. 'It is my plan to devote the rest of my life to sacrifice.'

'I mean —' Sango said. 'I – I wanted to say that I cannot accept your offer. I wish I could, but —'

'As you wish!' The Councillor waved his arm. 'You're under no obligation.'

'Thank you. I – I hope you win your seat.'

Sango was embarrassed and confused by Dele's stare of surprise. Once outside he breathed deeply, filling his lungs with air and slowly puffing it out.

'You surprise me, Sango.' Dele did not even wait to get out of earshot.

'It's simple. I like freedom. Not too much politics. Not too much moral guidance. You know the sort of life I lead. Jazz . . . girls . . . late hours. Odd assignments. Queer visitors at awkward times. I don't want to be too much under observation. It might change my character completely. At Twenty Molomo it's not like that.'

'I can't understand it,' Dele said. He tried to smile as he shook hands with Sango, but for once his acting ability failed him. He was sore as a child.

Since Bayo could not put through his plan at his own home, he decided to use Sango's room. He had called in the afternoon and Sango was out looking for a room; and now it was evening, and still Sango was out, which suited him.

'Come and open the door, please,' he told Sam. 'I want to sit down and wait for him . . . by the way, did a man with a black bag call here for me? Like a doctor.'

'Man with a black bag? I don' see anybody, sah.'

Very reluctantly, Sam opened the door. Bayo's hand trembled but he did not let Sam see it. Every time he thought of his get-rich-quick plan, his heart gave a leap of fear. Something might still go wrong. No, the nurse would not double-cross him. He was a reliable fellow.

'Sam, trust me. I shall steal nothing. I'll just play some music till my friend comes.'

'All right, sah. When you want to go, let me know.'

Bayo was impatient. He walked to the corridor, peered outside, came back. He could not sit still for one moment. He thumbed through a magazine, put it down, searched his pockets for cigarettes. There were none. He sat down again.

This could be a very dangerous business. The penicillin racket had made some people and broken others. He wished he had not posed as a doctor. He wished he had not told that old woman that penicillin would cure all her ills. But there was a matter of five guineas to be considered.

There was a knock and a man carrying a leather bag came into the room. He put his raincoat on the arm of a chair and sat facing the door. He was the 'nurse' whom Bayo had engaged to administer the drug.

The man said impatiently: 'Where's the woman? I thought you said eight-thirty. Well, it's time.'

'She'll soon be here. Give me a cigarette, please.'

'I don't trust this place. I don't know why, but I feel a bit scared.' The nurse glanced nervously round. 'Suppose she discovers I'm no nurse, but a quack?'

'Give me a cigarette.'

'I don't smoke.'

'You sound annoyed. Why, now?'

The nurse glanced about the room. At every footfall he rose and went to the door. 'I thought it was our patient . . .'

'She'll be bringing the whole five guineas,' Bayo said. 'She'll give me the money and we'll split it. You will have —'

'You will have one pound ten shillings. That's what we agreed, Bayo.'

'I'm having two-twelve-six!' Bayo said, his eyes flaring. 'But keep quiet. We don't want Sam to know what we're doing. If possible too, I don't want him to know what we've done. Sango is very queer. He may disapprove.'

They turned when they heard the knock. Aina's mother had entered the room. 'Where is . . . the other man? The one who lives here?' She sounded disappointed.

'Do you want the man, or do you want your medicine?'

Bayo asked. 'Don't worry about the man who lives here. Me and my friend will attend to you. My friend is a famous nurse.'

She looked about her suspiciously. 'I was here – once. When Aina fell into trouble.'

'You . . . must be Aina's mother? Lord save me!' Bayo did not like this new turn of events. So this woman knew that Sango lived here, knew perhaps that the racket was against the law. And with the painful plight of her daughter in mind, what could she not scheme?

'Five guineas, not so?' She fumbled in her cloth and produced a little envelope. 'Here is your money.'

Bayo and the nurse exchanged glances. It was the easiest thing ever. Ten cases like this, twenty cases, a hundred . . . and they would be rich. Bayo took the money from her, checked the notes expertly, almost contemptuously.

The woman rose. 'Excuse me, I've just remembered something. I'll be back just now.'

She was out of the room before they could stop her. Bayo and the nurse again exchanged an uneasy glance. Bayo went to the table, poured himself a glass of water. He raised it to his lips, then stopped. An idea had struck him. Suppose this woman did not return before Sango came back?

And then, by one of those odd things that happen once in a lifetime, Bayo in returning the glass to the table upset it. The water poured on the notes which the woman had given them in payment.

Immediately they became an intense violet. On the back of each note appeared the letters C.I.D.

'Nurse! We're finished. Betrayed! The woman has gone to call the police. Look, marked notes. Get your bag and let's run!'

Sango paid off his taxi at Twenty Molomo Street and got in quickly, hoping to rattle off the story of the *Apala* dance in good time to catch tomorrow's edition. He felt that he had stumbled on one of the mysteries of the city. This was

CYPRIAN EKWENSI

his chance to catch McMaster's attention with his handling of the assignment. Two women go to a dance, and while dancing one of them collapses and dies. There is no explanation. She has been in a state of elation before her sudden death. The dance has taken her into a kind of trance and she is foaming at the lips. Why? What is the significance? The more he thought of the woman's face, her eyes glazed, staring about her unseeing, her tongue lolling out of her mouth, the more terrified he became. Everyone had sat forward, waiting in suspense. They knew she was possessed. Even the drumming had ceased, and yet she continued to dance – without the music. He could never forget it.

The pathologist had said something about the woman 'at the time of her death . . . undue physical exertion . . . advanced state of myocardial degeneration . . . in the grip of an all-possessing emotion . . .' or some such jargon, very convenient but still leaving the mystery uncleared.

He glanced at his watch. It was past nine. The story could not possibly get through now for tomorrow's paper. In the corridor he met Sam carrying a cooking-pot and Sam told him: 'Your friend Bayo is here. Himself with some strangers. I think C.I.D.'

He stopped, his heart leaping into his mouth. What could he have done? He was no politician, or youth leader. He knocked at his own door and went in. Apart from Bayo, Sango could not say where he had seen the others before. One of them was slender and badly tailored. He had the air of a man on the verge of panic and his fever tended to be contagious. His trousers were greasy and unlined. He showed dirty teeth when he smiled. He held his card and Sango saw he was from the police.

'We are searching your room.'

Another man, robust, in dark sun-goggles even in the room, looked at his watch.

'We have found nothing in the room. Now I'm afraid we must search the clothes of the two gentlemen.'

56

Sango's heart sank. He saw Bayo close his eyes. The robust policeman patted the bulges on his dress.

'You're sure you haven't got them in your shoes?'

Sango slumped into the nearest seat. He heard the other policeman say, 'I've found something! On the floor!'

He was holding a note marked with the letters C.I.D. 'Who owns this?'

Bayo opened his eyes.

'I've never seen that before!'

'I must ask you both to come to the station,' the stout man said. 'Nothing much, just formalities.'

'Sorry about the inconvenience, Amusa . . .'

'You know my name!'

'Amusa Sango, crime reporter *West African Sensation.* The most eligible bachelor along Molomo Street. But take care women don't land you in trouble.' He showed his dirty teeth.

They went out.

Sango could not get his grip on things. He knew he must write his report but try as he would he could not concentrate.

Sam came into the room. 'Lajide is very annoyed with you, sah. He say he never get C.I.D. men in this house since he built it. He and the men talk for long time before they take Bayo away in the 999 van.'

'Not very good news, Sam; we don't want anything to annoy Lajide now.'

'Jus' so, sah. That Bayo is a bad boy. You better be careful of him, sah. He will put somebody in big trouble.'

'What d'you mean?'

'I will show you somethin', sah.'

Sam went out and in a moment returned with the cooking-pot which Sango had seen him carrying a moment ago. 'Master, look what they give me to take to barber and keep. I no meet barber in the shop . . .'

He opened the pot.

'What!' exclaimed Sango on seeing the hypodermic syringe

and the phials of penicillin. 'Go and throw that into the lagoon, quick! You want to put us all in prison?'

Carefully Sam wrapped the dangerous goods in paper, threw a cloth over his shoulder and stepped out into the street, whistling.

Sango did not find out the full details of this incident until, out of sheer habit, he dropped in at the All Language Club. It was past midnight and Sango felt entitled to the treat, since he had already dispatched his copy to Layeni, the night editor of the *Sensation*.

'Amusa Sango!' It was First Trumpet. He looked up from a music score as Sango entered the club. 'Where have you been? Since eight we have been waiting for you and now it's over midnight? Or you forgot?'

'I'm sorry, First Trumpet! You carry on. Lead the band for a change. Let me have an instrument.'

There was a clarinet which Sango took over; and, for the first time since he owned a band, he played sitting down. But his mind was not on his music. He was thinking generally of himself in the big city. What had he achieved? Where was he going? Was he drifting like the others, or had he a direction? Whatever that direction was, he did not feel at this moment that he was progressing along it. Certainly his mother would not be proud to see how he was making out. Crime reporter for the *West African Sensation*. Leader of a band in a night club. The old woman would think he was lost. As far as money was concerned, there was little of it being put aside for the rainy day; and then there were the girls, every one with her own problems and thrice as interesting as the last. Something must have happened to his noble resolutions.

The number was a hot one, and he rose and took a bouncing solo, registering the twisting, writhing bodies, the glittering jewellery, the shuffling feet and wiggling hips. He could smell the mixture of dust, perfume and sweat. The excitement rose to a rollicking climax topped with cheers. He looked up and saw his friend Bayo, just entering the Club and performing a late jig at the entrance.

During the interval, Bayo came and apologized for his irresponsible action. 'Sango, I didn't want you to know at all. I needed money, you know . . .'

'You were joking with a hundred pounds' fine or two years' imprisonment, or both, so the books say.'

'You know when they were searching me, I was shivering . . . I prayed and prayed. I was lucky they found nothing on me. You know what happened to the "nurse"? He was detained. No bail allowed.'

'You'd better learn your lesson, Bayo. If I find you mixing with any more of the underworld, I shall never have anything more to do with you. You have angered Lajide, my landlord. He is very annoyed. Sam told me.'

'Sango, I'm sorry. The mistake was mine. I did not know that woman was Aina's mother. She arranged with the police! What, the malice that woman has against you! You better be careful yourself. The trouble was not meant for me, but for you. I advise you to leave Twenty Molomo before they plan something else.'

'Aina's mother? Of course! But didn't you know? You were playing with fire. The first time I saw her I thought she was a witch. Honestly.'

'Where's the syringe?'

'Don't worry about that. It's safe.'

At that moment the band began to stir to life once more. Sango took himself off and went back. First Trumpet was mustering forces for a *Highlife. One, two!* and away it went, soft, lilting . . .

Molomo Street was dead. Gone were the lingering lovers under the almond trees. The water-pump in the street dripped unnoticed. Sango's steps were loud, clear and lonely. He turned into Number Twenty, a tired man.

The corridor was completely impassable. Arm-chairs, stools,

books and lino cluttered up the passage. At first Sango thought that a new tenant had just moved in. He got to his door and tried to open it. The key would not fit. It was only then that the truth dawned on him. He looked more closely at the furniture in the corridor. He recognized, with gradually increasing shock and anger, his own bookshelves, his own radio and gramophone.

Sam emerged from the gloom.

'Welcome, sah!'

'What's this, Sam?'

'I tol' you, Lajide is annoyed with you, sah. He remove all your thin' and put his wife in your room. I been to police office to report him, but he bribe everybody; they will do nothing.'

Sam handed Sango a note which he read by the glow of a distant light. It said simply: I FINISH WITH YOU.

Considering how involved the whole procedure would be in taking Lajide to court, and the risk of having the penicillin racket dug up all over again, Amusa decided to let sleeping dogs lie.

The door of his own room opened and one of Lajide's wives poked her head out.

'Too much noise. You won' let me sleep!'

Sango bit his lip to keep back the torrent of angry words. 'I don't blame you – but don't rejoice too soon. You will be the next one in the corridor – and you will never come back!'

7

As far as Sango was concerned, Beatrice could not have chosen a worse time to call at Twenty Molomo. This girl, whom he had wanted to impress with his importance and charm, dismissed her taxi in front of Lajide's house and stepped delicately into the courtyard. A wide-brimmed straw hat with trailing ribbons framed her face. Her eyes were hidden by the latest fad in glasses, silver-rimmed and so flattering that Sango stood confused and unable to fathom the eyes behind the dark shields. Her cool blue frock moulded a body that cried out to be wooed and she carried a black bag, while the gloves summarized her sophistication.

It was impossible that Beatrice had failed to notice the *omolanke* or hand-cart which stood outside while Sam loaded his master's possessions on to it. It was common knowledge in the city that your method of shifting lodgings depended on your means. A poor man employed head porters; a man of average means hailed the hand-carts and trailed behind them with the more precious things. But a man who had posed as a bandleader would naturally be expected to go one step better and engage a lorry.

Beatrice had stretched out her hand, and as Sango took it she smiled, and said: 'At last, I've found it. I was trying to follow your description from the All Language Club.'

'I see! Welcome. It's not all that difficult —'

'For someone always locked up in Rokiya Hill it's not so easy.' She seemed then to notice the cluttered-up passage.

CYPRIAN EKWENSI

'Are these your things? You are not packing? No, of course, you would have used a car . . .'

'I've been thrown out, Beatrice.'

He caught the breath of her perfume and it went to his head. 'I'm not all that well off, Beatrice. And as you've chosen to come at such an awkward time, I can offer you no hospitality.'

'All right! Let me go and see Lajide. Wish me luck!'

She smiled and walked up the stairs. He was watching her swinging hips. Suddenly he felt angry at the way he was getting on in the city. Something must be done about it soon, for he was certain now that the good things were eluding him. He was actually getting nowhere, come to think of it. He was still crime reporter, *West African Sensation*, and band-leader at the All Language Club. If that was status, then he must be sadly mistaken.

Beatrice had been offered a seat in Lajide's sitting-room. One look at the carpets, the expensive curtains, the large pictures and ebony carvings, had confirmed her first impression. This was a man who loved finery. He was not likely to be stingy in spending money on a woman he fancied. He was not economical either, or he would not leave the fluorescent lights on in the room. The window blinds had been tactfully drawn, lending a touch of enchanting glamour and romantic isolation to the room. She had to remind herself that it was afternoon, and hot. This was the reception-room of a man who might be called upon to make love at short notice by any of eight women. A glance in the mirror revealed that her spider-web of a dress had acquired a new and dazzling colour reflected by the lights. This was the sort of setting that made her most seductive.

Lajide came into the room as she was sitting down. He threw himself into a couch and stared at her with no attempt to hide his admiration. Even as he sat down, one of his wives, Alikatu, came into the room, carrying a large bowl of some aromatic fluid. She set it down and eyed Beatrice with all the venom of a possible rival and disappeared, no doubt to go and gossip with the others.

It has started, Beatrice thought. She has already come to assess me. I am a woman and I understand.

Lajide sipped the fluid. 'Welcome, Madam. What can I do for you?'

'I'm looking for a room.'

'Oh. What happen to the ol' one?'

'I'm not happy there . . .'

'Finish? You're not happy there, so you want to leave? Come on, tell me the truth! You have quarrelled with your husband, not so? *Omashe-O!*' He shook his head.

'Not that,' Beatrice protested. 'It is not healthy for me. I'm always sick there. I suspect somebody is trying to poison me, so I wan' to leave the place.'

In his eyes she saw the brightening glow of desire. His face looked crafty; his lips twisted with a smile. 'If I give you room, you will be my woman?' He rose, opened a nearby cupboard, produced a bottle and two small glasses. He walked to the centre of the room, poured and downed a drink; then poured her one. 'I like you; I like you very much.'

She took the drink, but his hand trembled so that it spilled on the floor. The fire in his eyes had settled into a steady glow, undisguisable. She could feel the almost boundless passion of the man: an insatiable lust that made him lord of eight women.

'You like me . . . what of your wives? I don't want any trouble.' She sipped her drink and found it was whisky, very welcome in her present mood.

'Never mind about them. You have your room. I won't stop you from anything, but you must be my woman. You will be free, and live outside. You hear me. I will keep you outside; you won't mix with the others – here. Don't bother about the rent . . .'

The terms were worth considering.

Lajide moved closer so she could smell his thick whisky

breath. He must have been drinking the whole day. 'When I say a room, I mean a good room. You see, is no good living in a hole; no, not girl like you. One Lebanese is coming to see me this night about my fine house at Clifford Street. I will give you a room from there. What say you?'

'Do you want a reply now?'

Lajide shrugged. 'As you like. People are rushing for the house . . . I can reserve one room for you, but if you waste time —' He waved his arm, the arm of the giver and the taker.

'Reserve a room for me, Lajide. But I'll think of the other part.'

'What you have to think about? Is not many women I will say, I want you to be my woman, and they begin think. Fancy that!'

'Perhaps my husband will like to see you about the room first.' Beatrice smiled very sweetly.

Lajide's face drained of colour. 'Your husband! That's all right! That's all right, I don't worry. Come, I take you home in my car.' He reached for his bunch of keys.

Beatrice hesitated.

'Come now —'

'Just a minute, Mr Lajide. That young man downstairs, Mr Amusa Sango. What did he do to you?'

'Leave him alone. He's a very bad young man. I give him notice long time, then he want to put me in trouble. He bring C.I.D. men here. Better for him to go now in peace before big trouble meet him in my house.'

'Can't you give him a room in your new house?'

Lajide's mouth opened in surprise. '*Me?*' and he laughed.

Down the stairs Beatrice went, with the man in the voluminous robes trailing close behind her. She noticed that the corridor was now clear and that Sango was gone. Lajide was talking incessantly, about his wealth, his influence in the city, and the stupidity of certain tenants.

At the door of Twenty Molomo a maroon car of American make, streamlined, with chromium streaks, glided to a stop nodding proudly. The door opened and a Lebanese in a white shirt and shorts slid out.

Lajide whispered to Beatrice: 'Tha's the man who want to buy my new house.' He raised his voice: 'Hello, Muhammed Zamil . . . I just goin' out.'

'Lajide, is the house ready?'

'Almost ready.'

'Every day almost ready; every day almost ready —'

'I want to do fine job; have patience, you will like the place when I finish.'

'Is all right for me now.'

'*Oya!*' said Lajide suddenly. 'Let's go now. We see the house, then you sign!'

Finishing touches were being put to the house at 163B Clifford Street West. The painters, electricians and carpenters had been working hard in the last few weeks. It was painted in a sun- and rain-resisting cream on the outside, the inner walls in a very pale green. The garage was spacious enough to take Zamil's car without its tail preventing the doors from closing. There were quarters for the 'small boy', cook and steward.

Beatrice thought it was a much more useful house than the one she shared with Grunnings on Rokiya Hill. But where in all this scheme did she fit in? She decided not to accept a room here, if Lajide gave her one. She might just as well be Zamil's mistress.

Zamil got into his car, and held the door open for Beatrice to come in and sit beside him. And there she sat between two men, each trying to please her, while her mind dwelt on Amusa Sango and his plight.

They drove into a side street and Zamil who had been showing signs of impatience burst out: 'What's matter, is this Clifford Street?'

'We go and see my solicitor. Have patience!'

CYPRIAN EKWENSI

Lajide drew his pouch, selected a cigarette and lit it. 'You want the house, or you don't want the house? Ah-ah! I never see hot temper man like you. If you don't want the house any more, let me go back!'

'I'm sorry, Lajide. I thought —'

'Park your car and follow me. Beatrice, you wait for us.'

She watched them go up a narrow lane. When they emerged a long time afterwards, smelling faintly of alcohol, the agreement to lease 163B had been signed, sealed and delivered.

Beatrice heard Lajide say: 'The house will be your own for five years now.'

He took out a cheque from his pocket-book and looked at it once more. He acted like a man slightly tipsy, waving it in Beatrice's face and saying with his drunken breath: 'Five thousand pounds on this paper. Ha!'

Zamil said: 'Lajide, we must celebrate. I want you to come with me for a bite – anywhere.'

He drove to the department store by the lagoon. Gingerly Beatrice walked along the pavement between the two men. As usual the snack bar was crowded with people of the city out to relax and look at the lagoon. They were mostly girls of the Dupeh type, fashion plates of the most devastating type – to young men. With every swing of the doors, the restaurant filled more than it emptied.

They sat down and made their orders. Beatrice could see at once that Lajide felt ill-at-ease, and shortly after the steward had taken their orders he begged to be excused.

'I'll see you later, Beatrice. I got business at home.'

Beatrice looked up and saw a man, notebook in hand, just coming in through the swing doors. It was Amusa Sango. He had not seen her. Her heart fluttered till she was giddy.

'Is a big day for me,' came Zamil's voice beside her. She was not listening. 'Name anything you like downstairs in the shop and is yours . . .'

The waiter arrived with a tray full of orders for three. Beatrice looked beyond the waiter and saw that Amusa had come in with a girl. Who was she? She could not see the face behind the make-up and sunshade.

'I must leave you now,' and she got up, smiling, and walked across the restaurant conscious of admiring eyes. Sango looked up as she approached.

'Beatrice!'

She took the only vacant seat next to Sango, beaming happily. 'What brings you here?'

'You want to hear my hard-luck story? Well, I couldn't find a place in the city. My work has to go on, so what did I do? I took my things to the railway station and deposited them in the Left Luggage Office, and here I am!'

'And your boy – what did you do with him?'

'Sam has gone back to his younger brother. His brother is a trader. Lives in a tiny room just off Twenty Molomo. I'm sorry I had to lose him, but —' He shrugged his shoulders.

'Amazing! Do you sleep at the station, too?'

'Not yet. I'm now a hanger-on till I can find a place. My First Trumpet has invited me to share his little room with him.'

'Is not easy,' Beatrice said, and told him how Lajide wanted her to be his woman.

'When you're a man,' Sango said, 'they want six months' or a year's rent in advance. When you're an attractive woman, single, or about to be single, they want you as a mistress. That's the city.'

'What am I to do, Sango?'

'If I were not engaged, I would say, marry me. As it is, I can only advise you to stick to Grunnings. He's much nicer than either of those two men – Lajide or Zamil. He's responsible, at least.' He stopped when he noted her obvious disappointment. He looked at her and felt a strong desire to protect her as a woman in danger.

'I don't know what to do with my life,' she said. She glanced round nervously as if to see if anyone had overheard.

Sango said, 'Let's go somewhere quiet and you can tell

me about it. Do you mind if we pass by the offices of the *West African Sensation*? I have a report to hand in to the editor.'

'I don't mind, Sango. But where's the girl with you?'

'Disappeared. Don't worry. She was just a pick-up.' He folded his notebook, paid his bill. Together they walked through the thick cigarette fumes. He was flattered by her loyalty to him.

They passed by Zamil's table and he looked up in surprise. Once out by the lagoon, they found a park bench under a coconut palm looking out at the ships anchored in the lagoon. A woman with a child strapped to her back was buying fish from a canoeman. Near by a man was dragging his nets out of the lagoon and pouring hundreds of silvery little fish into a canoe.

Beatrice talked freely, with little interruption from Sango. He listened, and as her story unfolded he asked himself: what is the secret of getting ahead in the city? Beatrice had disclosed that she came to the city from the Eastern Greens, from the city of coal. She made no secret of what brought her to the city: 'high life.' Cars, servants, high-class foods, decent clothes, luxurious living. Since she could not earn the high life herself, she must obtain it by attachment to someone who could. But she was not so well, and having found Grunnings, who did not quite satisfy her, she had to stick to him.

'But I'm tired of him and want to leave. But should I agree to what Lajide suggests? I do not like him very much.'

Sango thought it over. His mind was confused. Her total trust in him had diverted his original desire for her. He could think of her now only as a sister. He forgot that he ever wanted her.

What he was too blind to see was that Beatrice had fallen in love with him. He talked to her about sticking to Grunnings and she looked only into his eyes and held his hand with tenderness.

Then he realized that she was not listening and had started dozing in the soft sea breeze.

Day by day thousands of copies of the *West African Sensation* rolled off the huge presses, were quickly bundled into waiting green vans that immediately struck out north, east, west, covering the entire country from the central point of the city. In the last few months of his present tour, McMaster's policy of giving local writers free rein was beginning to pay off. The *West African Sensation* was becoming a part of life, something eagerly awaited for its stories of politics, crime, sport, and entertainment.

For Sango, life had settled down to a routine and he seemed to be looking for some excitement to brighten up his page. Sometimes he had to remind himself that however exciting crime was, it brought tragedy to someone. But it was his function to report it, and to him it had become something clinical, with neither blood nor sentiment attached.

Unexpectedly, his chance came one afternoon with a strange phone call; and it very nearly altered his whole life. The caller had said that a body had been found floating on the lagoon. McMaster had instantly detailed Sango to cover the assignment.

Sango found on his arrival at the beach that a huge crowd had gathered in the manner of the people of the city. The police vans blared at them through loudspeakers, urging them to keep clear and to touch nothing. The shops and offices had emptied and there were clerks with pencils stuck to their ears, fashionable girls with baskets of shopping slung over their arms, ice-cream hawkers pedalling bicycles, motorists tooting their horns. The coconut palms waved their lazy fronds over the body draped in white and lying on the sands.

Sango went over and took a bold look at the face. It was the body of a man in the prime of life, and, as it turned out later, he had taken his own life. His name, Sango discovered, was Buraimoh Ajikatu. He had been missing from home for about three days. He was a clerk in a big department store and he was married, with four children.

They said he had been finding it increasingly difficult to support his family. To him the city had been an enemy that raised the prices of its commodities without increasing his pay; or even when the pay was increased, the increased prices immediately made things worse than before.

Buraimoh's plight was not alleviated by a nagging wife. He complained aloud and a friend at the office who worked no harder but always enjoyed the good things of life, said: 'Have you not heard of the *Ufemfe* society?'

He had not heard and the friend told him about Lugard Square at midnight. There was to be a meeting. He went, and was enrolled. They promised him all he wanted. And strangely enough, life became bearable. He could not understand why his salary was increased, or why he was promoted to stores assistant, but it was not in his place to question. There was even a promise of becoming branch manager within one month. Why had it not happened all the time he was not an *Ufemfe* member? That too he could not answer. But he had been initiated and he now knew the secret sign of *Ufemfe*; this revealed to him that he had been the only non-member in the department store.

One night the blow fell. This was the unexplained portion of the pact. They asked him in a matter-of-fact manner to give them his first-born son. He protested, asked for an alternative sacrifice, and when they would not listen threatened to leave the society. But they told him that he could not leave. There was a way in, but none out – except through death. He was terrified, but adamant.

He had told no one of his plight, and that was when he vanished from home. Now that the good things of life were his, he would not go back and tell his wife. All this Sango learnt, and much more besides. For him it had great significance. By uncovering this veil, he had discovered where all the depressed people of the city went for sustenance. They literally sold their souls to the devil.

Even so, when things became much too unbearable for him, Sango often thought it would not be the worst thing in life to join the *Ufemfe*. And he would remember that swollen body with its protruding tongue and bulging eyes, a body that had been rescued from the devil's hands and given a decent Christian burial. And yet the tragedy remained.

8

Sango had heard of the coal crisis which broke out in the Eastern Greens, of the twenty-one miners who had been shot down by policemen under orders from 'the imperialists'. To him it had a faint echo of something happening in a distant land.

He was somewhat taken aback when McMaster called him into the office and told him that a passage had been booked for him to travel to the Eastern Greens and bring back reports.

Sango was not happy to leave the city where he was still unsettled, sharing a room with First Trumpet, having his meals outside. But worse still he was afraid he might see his mother and find her worse than ever. He had just sent her twelve pounds – all the money he had kept to deposit as advance payment for a room.

The plane was taking him towards the Eastern Greens, nearer the source of his poverty, of his ambition to seek his fortune as a journalist and musician west of the Great River. Until he landed and visited the mines and saw the scene of desolation he could think of nothing else but his mother in hospital, and the girl Elina in the convent. He would try, if possible, to visit the two of them. It did not seem possible to visit the two places in the little time that would be available.

He saw the Great River below, broad and brownish with here and there a canoeman – a mere dot many thousands of feet below. Instantly his past life seemed to flash before his eyes. He saw his own poverty and his youthful ambition and found that he must work still harder to give happiness to his dependants.

As the plane touched down Sango saw the expectant group standing at the air terminal. One of them would be Mr Nekam, President of the Workers' Union. Sango had not met him but had seen pictures of him in the *Sensation*. Indeed Nekam was there, bearded and in a bush shirt.

'You'll be staying with me,' he said to Sango, shaking him warmly by the hand. 'So, better you cancel your hotel booking.'

Sango, who wanted to see both sides of the dispute, told Nekam: 'You'll give me a free hand, I hope; not try to influence my reports in any way.'

They drove through unmade roads into the workers' quarters and Sango noted immediately the atmosphere one experiences in a town under the iron boot. Policemen were everywhere. Not the friendly unarmed men he had been used to in the city, but aggressive boot-stamping men who carried short guns, rifles or tear-gas equipment. There were African police and white officers and they all had that stern killer look on their faces. The shadow of death had darkened the people's faces as they went about their daily business, and though Sango listened hard, he could hear no laughter.

He decided to go – not to the president's house – but to the famous valley of death at the foot of the hills where the coal was mined. Here he saw the thorn scrub where many wounded miners had crawled in agony to die of bullet wounds. At the Dispensary many of the miners were being treated for head injuries and fractures in thigh and arm.

Sango spoke to them and their story was full of lament. They told how an outstanding allowance, amounting to thousands of pounds, had been denied them. How frequently labour disputes arose, and how the mine boss – an overbearing white man – would not listen. The background to the shooting had been simply – strained feelings.

Back in the home of the workers' president, Sango found

that Nekam occupied a little compound with two rooms and one kitchen, that his wife raised chickens and rented a stall in the market where she sold cigarettes, tinned foods and cloth. The children had been sent away into the village because of the emergency.

Sango got down immediately to work. Nekam showed him copies of telegrams from the West African Students' Union in London, the President of the Gold Coast, the League of Coloured Peoples in New York . . . and one from a President in South America, urging Nekam to bring the matter up at the United Nations. Some of the telegrams were unrealistic but heartening.

At a Press conference the following day, Sango discovered that this shooting had become a cementing factor for the nation. The whole country, north, east, and west of the Great River, had united and with one loud voice condemned the action of the British Government in being so trigger-happy and hasty. Rival political parties had united in the emergency and were acting for the entire nation. Sango was thrilled.

In his report he was loud in praise of the new movement and caustic in his comment on the attitude of the British. His youthful fire knew no restraint and he wrote about the bleeding and the dying, the widowed and the homeless; the necessity to compensate these men who had sacrificed so much that the country's trains might run, its power-houses function, and its industries flourish. No other correspondent had been so brave and forthright, and the *Sensation* was eagerly bought and read for 'the real truth about the coal crisis in the Eastern Greens'.

For Sango the great question was: why do politicians have to wait for a period of crisis before they can sink their selfish differences and unite? Why can it not always be like this, what can we do to hold this new feeling? Even as he tortured himself with these questions he knew that as soon as the crisis was over the leaders would all go their different and opposite ways, quarrelling like so many market women.

At night he was at the airport to see the arrival of dark troop-planes from Great Britain. His report on the arrival of these reinforcements drew forth an immediate denial from the Government. The troops had nothing to do with the coal crisis, they said. And now the coal city was drained of women and children, black and white. Only the able-bodied men remained to face the terror.

Thanks to the unity of the politicians a way out was found. In the leaders Nekam placed all his confidence. In him the workers, in their turn, believed. The result was that the politicians said to Nekam:

'We must do things in a constitutional manner. It is hard, but that is the best sign of maturity. We don't want any more demonstrations or violence. Go and get your miners back to work and leave all negotiations with the British to us. Do we represent you or do we not? That is the first question.'

'You do!' grunted Nekam.

Nekam, who had faith in the politicians, told the workers, who surely still had faith in him. He spent all night negotiating with the gang leaders who accused him of back-pedalling. By early morning he was fagged out. He invited Sango to the railway station where the workers took their train. If they did return to work, his task had been performed. If they did not, then something else must be tried; he could not now tell what.

They stood looking down at the valley below. The mist of morning cleared from the hills. In the east the sky reddened and the redness oozed into the valley. Sango peered, then held Nekam excitedly. Nekam followed Sango's eyes, but said nothing. His lips were pursed. Down there, there was movement – in groups. Neither Sango nor Nekam dare say the groups were composed of miners coming to work. It was best to wait. Soon the train would come.

The first man arrived with pick and Davy lamp, followed by others and soon the station was humming with mumbling men. They had come. He had succeeded. With hearts too full

75

for words, Sango and Nekam boarded the train which took them down to the mines.

Sango followed them inside, into the abyss of the earth where heat reigned supreme, and reverberations threatened the teak props. There was ever present a sense of death, danger, disaster. Yet the men who risked all worked in sweat and courage.

Sango heard a rumbling ahead of him and went forward to investigate. The gang leader pulled him back. 'Look out! Coal coming up!'

Sango stepped aside, just in time. A chain of automatic wagons loaded with coal clattered by. The striking miners had produced the first fruits of their toil and of Nekam's negotiations.

That same afternoon, a telegram was delivered to Sango. He tore it open with blackened hands. Nekam was peering over his shoulder.

COME BACK BY LORRY STOP YOU CAN GET FAST SERVICE FROM JIKAN TRANSPORT STOP REGARDS MCMASTER

'You going back?' Nekam said.
'The job is done, isn't it?'

Daybreak found Sango and Nekam at the lorry station. Knowing how 'fast' the lorry service could be from the Eastern Greens, Sango made sure that the driver of Jikan Transport would stop in the village near the convent where Elina was. It would be a good opportunity to see her.

While the lorry was being loaded up with passengers, dried fish, yams and oil, Nekam talked of his ambitions to see the country progress as a whole till it took its place in the front rank of self-governing countries within the British Commonwealth. There was still a lot to be done, but this crisis was only the beginning of national unity.

'Keep up the struggle, Sango. We workers at this end will never give up.'

Sango had listened to this kind of serious talk once before:

that bright day when he had been at an identical motor station, and his father, an old man, now no more, had come to see him off. The hairy Nekam was less gentle, more full of fire.

The lorry horned. 'That's the signal to go aboard, Nekam. Thank you for your hospitality. You've made me see the whole business from the inside as a real reporter should. I'd like you to be a little patient. I'm sure the National Committee for Justice which the politicians have formed will do something. The bereaved will get full social compensation. And when the Commission of Inquiry arrives from Britain, I hope I shall be here again to listen to the evidence.'

Nekam stood back, while Sango walked towards the lorry and took a seat in the second class – a little partition shielded from the driver. He sat with his knees bunched up, counting the miles between him and the village where Elina was.

The lorry backed away and there stood Nekam under a tree, his arm raised. Sango waved back. It had taken a national disaster of the magnitude of shooting down twenty-one unarmed men to bring together leaders from north, east and west, to make the country realize as never before where its real destiny lay. What catastrophe, Sango wondered, would crystallize for him the direction of his own life? Soon – perhaps in another twelve months – he might be called upon to marry Elina; certainly his mother would insist on this to protect him from the gold-digging women of the city. But would he be ready?

A fat woman sitting on his right sighed. He turned and looked at her face, radiant and attractive. Before the lorry had moved three miles, she was fast asleep, using Sango's back as a pillow.

When the lorry at last pulled up at the little village, Sango found that his second-class seat had been worth having after all. The other passengers in the third class were covered from head to foot in red dust.

The convent was beautifully situated: about a mile or two

from the main motor-road, it overlooked an arm of the river. Sango walked across the village and beyond the market-place till he was well out in the woods. Peace and quiet such as he could never dream of, were here in the scented air, and the music of unseen birds. It was incredible, this idealized setting which had been chosen for a convent. Less than a hundred miles from the scene of death, desolation and the shattering of amities, yet this place stubbornly refused to see the evil in the world, talked only of the good and the pure. The sadness came when the girls graduated, as Elina would. Then rude shocks were theirs in the words, thoughts and deeds of the outside world.

Sango's steps were already becoming reluctant. He knew before the gate swung back and admitted him that some purification treatment must be meted out to him before he could dream of being worthy of Elina.

One of the girls led him round the beautifully kept lawns to the waiting-room, where she showed him a school bench and told him to wait. It was siesta time, she explained, and Elina must not be disturbed. Sango, confronted with pictures of the Madonna and Child, the Sacred Heart of Jesus radiating mercy to sinners like himself, saw no hope of his own salvation. He knelt down suddenly and made the sign of the cross.

At that moment he vowed to spend the rest of his life doing good, and cared nothing for the fact that the lorry-driver up at the village had told him as he poured palm-wine into his drinking horn: 'Don' keep long.'

It took some time before a delicate rustle startled Sango out of his reverie. The Mother Superior, for she it must be, in her whites and black hood, clear-skinned and graceful in her old age, came into the little waiting room.

'You sent a letter some time ago from the coal city? It is an awkward time to come, for the girls are at rest.'

Sango could see numerous heads peering into the room from dormitory windows. Such a commotion did a male visitor cause in a girls' establishment.

He said, 'Yes, Mother Superior.'

'But I'll treat this as a special case, since you live so far away.' Once again she questioned him about his name, religion, and occupation. She talked at length about Elina and, sweeping up her robe to avoid dust, she walked gently down the steps. Sango looked into the dormitory windows: the heads had vanished.

Elina was a tall girl, quick-smiling, but somewhat gawky in appearance. Looking at her as she hung timidly on the arm of the head-girl who led her in, Sango felt his heart contract with pain and disillusionment. Pure she must be, innocent, a virgin no doubt; but one whom Sango could never see himself desiring. He smiled back at her, hoping she could not by some mysterious means fathom his thoughts. He cursed himself for his city background which had taught him to appreciate the voluptuous, the sensual, the sophisticated in woman. Elina was none of these. What did he want for a wife, anyway? A whore? Perhaps not; but he knew what he did not want. This must be the most awkward moment of his life. He was tongue-tied, and the presence of a chaperone choked back any warmth he might have shown.

On the other hand this was a beautiful moment, full of significance for them both. He was the man from the city who would one day be her husband. She was the pure girl, brought up according to the laws of God and the Church, unadulterated and therefore totally ignorant of the realities of life, looking forward to a life divine with him. Could anything be more impossible, he asked himself?

How the interview ended he never could tell, but he found himself walking back across the village to the impatient lorry, now on the point of departing without him. Now something had gone out of his life's purpose. As an ideal, unseen and alive only in his imagination, Elina had been an incentive. But now he felt that urge gone. He was alone with no idealized plan. And there was his weakness for the city woman with no

restraining factor, nothing to check his lasciviousness. Whatever happened he was determined that his mother must not
know of his disappointment.

If only this lorry journey were ten times as long, he would
have time to work it all out before returning to the city.

PART TWO

When all doors are closed

9

This was no homecoming, because even though the taxi stopped in the lane where he shared a little room with First Trumpet, he had no feeling of ownership, let alone of freedom and privacy.

First Trumpet was dressed to go out, and in the band's uniform too. 'Ha, Sango, welcome!' He was polishing his trumpet. 'How you left us like that?'

And before Sango could answer: 'We read all your dispatches in the *Sensation*. But were you not afraid? That was hot news! How was the rioting out there?'

Sango put down his box in a corner and flopped into a chair. 'That's the first time I've relaxed in two weeks! Where are you going, all dressed up like this?'

'You've forgotten about the elections! Our band is playing for one of the parties. I don't care about their politics, but they pay well. Don't you see how I've been running the band in your absence?'

'Very good indeed.' He yawned. 'Well done! So I'm back with parties again. I thought we'd finished with parties as from last week. What's the use of all this nonsense when we are being led by the National Committee for Justice? I hope this election does not create a split. I'd hate to see the politicans split up once again.'

First Trumpet had his instrument under his arm and one foot on the doorstep. 'No . . . have no fear. They'll remain together, they won't split. You know how they act at election time. They make foolish promises, they abuse themselves. It's politics. Well! I must be off to Lugard Square; the band will be waiting.'

'Whom did you say you were playing for?'

'The S.G.N. Party.' He was already on the street.

Sango knew the S.G.N. (Self-Government-Now) Party as the one which claimed to represent the interests of the working man. Most of its members were people like Mr Nekam of the Eastern Greens. They were fanatics in their cause, and strongly opposed to the R.P. – the Realization Party – which helped people 'realize their dreams'.

Sango wished Sam were here to help him unpack his suitcase. First Trumpet had gone without even asking him whether he had had a meal recently. It was not strictly his business, but it would have been comforting to hear. Sango set about having a bath and a change of clothing. When he returned to his room, he found Bayo sitting in an armchair, a warm smile on his face.

'Sango! Ah-ah! You just flew away like that! This your job is terrible. But what have you been eating in that place? Your skin looks so fresh!'

Sango's heart warmed. Now he knew he was really back. 'I have plenty of news for you, Sango. Just wait. A lot has happened. Do you know, I saw your gal – the one who went to jail.'

'Aina?' Sango was thrilled to hear her name, the very mention of it. In one reckless moment, he forgot the pain of Elina. When he saw that Bayo had observed his eagerness, he feigned anger. But Bayo smiled.

'I saw her on Beecroft Bridge, selling cigarettes.'

'Oh?'

'But Sango, you don't sound interested. What's wrong? You're not like your old self. Or is the suffering you saw there still with you? Forget it, man!'

'I'm my old self, Bayo. It's nothing.'

He was putting on his cleanest shirt and selecting his best

tie. Why, he asked himself? Why? Must he impress an ex-jailbird like Aina? 'You have no feeling,' she had once told him.

'I don't blame you, anyway,' said Bayo. 'Those policemen are wicked. Shooting down their own brothers like that! Just because they wanted to be paid extra money. They'll not die well!'

He rambled on in his usual manner and soon the hard-luck story came up. 'I too, have changed. D'you know ... Don't you see how thin I have become?'

Sango looked at him. If there was anything thin about Bayo that evening it was the colour of his tie. His hair was permed as usual and the nylon ankle-socks that peeped out under the narrow trousers were ablaze with colour. The basket shoes had three tones.

'Sango, I've suffered too much in this world, and now I have made a decision. I made it when you were away, because I had no other friend in the world. Look, I said to myself. Bayo, everybody is becoming something. Our country is fighting for self-government. Our boys and girls are going to Britain and America, they are learning new things to make our country greater. I must become a serious man and move with the times.'

Sango looked at the face of his faithful friend. 'Do you really mean that, Bayo?'

Bayo sat forward with a show of indignation. 'Only the other day a lady bought me a new suit and gave me ten pounds on top. She is about forty-five, very wealthy, but no child. She has married, thrice, but no children. She wanted me to fulfil her desire, but I refused.'

'True, you mean that?'

It was certainly surprising for Bayo to act in this manner. Something must have happened. Sango was quite sure now. It could be the encounter with the police; but something must have happened. Bayo was restless, unable to sit still. He got up, went to the door, came back.

'I don't know why things always happen like this. I've gone out with a lot of girls; they've spent pots of money on me. Yet I never spend one mite on them; it doesn't pay to do so. All those girls were nothing to me —'

'What are you talking about, Bayo?'

'Do you know a girl called Suad Zamil? She's a Lebanese, sister of a cloth merchant.'

'Never heard of her. What's she to you?'

'I want to marry her; we've fixed everything for next month.'

'Does she love you?'

'You don't appear surprised, Sango. That's why I like you. You do not blame me when I make a mistake. Have I made a mistake? Tell me, Sango. Everyone is blaming me. They say the marriage is impossible between me, an African, and this Suad, a Lebanese. Do you know, Sango, what frightens me is that the girl cannot sit down or think or even eat or sell her brother's cloth in the shop, she's thinking of Bayo – oh my love! She is always at the window. I pass there one hundred times in one day and it is still not enough for her. She is not afraid of African food. She says she is prepared to eat even sand with me and if necessary live in our slum. Anywhere, so long I'm there. Do you think she is mad?'

'D'you love her?'

'Why d'you think I've been racking my brain in the last few weeks? Why d'you think I've been trying to make money on my own? Only you were not in town to advise me, that's what saddened me.'

Sango laced his shoes. This was one of those blinding love affairs into which Bayo was always falling, only to forget them entirely in a matter of days. He listened without attaching any importance to the words, and this attitude only made Bayo strive to impress him with his seriousness.

'She's the most beautiful girl in the whole world, and oh, so gentle! About nineteen, I should say, with very thick hair. You'll like to run your fingers through her hair, Sango. She does not speak any English, so we speak Yoruba. Yes, she's a native. She was born here . . .'

Bayo relapsed into a moody silence. Sango, who had finished dressing, said, 'Aina! Where can I find her?'

'Beecroft Bridge. As soon as you cross the bridge, look among the cigarette sellers. You'll see her.'

Beecroft Bridge was at least half a mile long. No one would sell cigarettes on the bridge, so Sango looked in the stalls outside the taxi park. It was already getting late and the shops were closing. Sango bade good-bye to Bayo on the bus and got down near the bridge. He began to search for Aina among the handful of girls selling cigarettes, but in this rush-hour din he could identify none of them. He had become a target for the final appeals of the late hawkers.

'Penny bread! . . . Sugar bread! . . .' they cried from all sides of him. He was irritated but trapped. '*Banjo*' (auction) '*akowe*' (envelopes) '*Banjo, akowe! . . .*'

The cars and lorries and buses were trying to press forward in the slow traffic-stream by tooting horns. 'Pip-pip! Paw-paw!'

Sango wanted to escape. He glanced desperately about him. Slippered feet rushed among the traffic, yet none belonged to the girl he sought. And the drone of the heavy diesel engines threatened to drown his voice.

Suddenly, everything seemed to stop, as if by an order. At that moment Sango caught just one glimpse: a girl straining upwards, trying to sell cigarettes to passengers through a bus window. He crossed the street, breaking through the tormenting chains that bound him prisoner.

'Aina!'

Her face was flushed with excitement, and she turned and looked into his eye. The change she was offering to the passenger on the bus slipped and rolled between the wheels. The cloth tied round her hips broke loose. Sango in one leap stood beside her.

She was panting with wonder. 'What do you want? Twenty years is not for ever. Did you think I would die in jail?'

'Let us go to the Hollywood, Aina. I'll call a taxi and we'll go and eat. Where's your stall? Have you anyone to look after it for you?'

It was a way of life she liked. The glamorous surroundings, the taxis, the quick drinks. This was one reason why she had come to the city from her home sixty miles away: to ride in taxis, eat in fashionable hotels, to wear the *aso-ebi*, that dress that was so often and so ruinously prescribed like a uniform for mournings, wakings, bazaars, to have men who wore white collars to their jobs as lovers, men who could spend.

'I can't. I —'

'You must, Aina! After all, this meeting calls for some celebration. We may become enemies after that, but just let me give you this welcome. After all, I've been away and returned only this afternoon. How was I to know that you had come out of —'

A taxi drew alongside. He said: 'The Hollywood!'

They were in and he was sitting beside her. Suddenly all the restraint he had imposed on himself broke loose and he held her in his arms and hugged her. She pushed against him like a naughty child, but he saw the tears in her eyes and he was sad. Yet the next moment she was laughing, teasing him derisively till all the pent-up desire he had for her broke over him and he knew he was still putty in her hands, this street walker with the dark, smooth face and white smile. Could it be for her sake that Elina had ceased to appeal to him? What was the magic of this unbreakable spell?

Outside the hotel he paid his fare and took her upstairs to the restaurant. He chose a seat near two large mirrors where Aina could have ample scope to admire her reflection. He tried to find out what the prison had taught her. She was bitter against him, that he could see. But she was also bitter against everybody, against the very city that had condemned her. She had become hardened. Where previously Aina might have stalled or hesitated, or used a tactful word, she now spoke bluntly. Amusa was shocked by her cynicism.

'It's money I want now,' she said.

He nodded understandingly.

'I'm coming to visit you, Amusa, so get some money ready.'

His heart sank. 'Er . . . Lajide sacked me . . . er —'

'Said he doesn't want thieves and jailbirds, like me – eh? Don't deny, I know!'

He swallowed. She had got him wrong, but why reveal to her his present address?

'Well, I'm a thief! I've been to jail, and I'll still come to Twenty Molomo Street, and I shall visit you! Nobody can stop me, not even Lajide!'

Sango looked round nervously. 'People are listening, Aina —'

'I don't care!' The waiter was standing behind her. Sango ordered chicken stew with rice.

There could be no guarantee that it did her any good, because throughout the meal she kept stabbing at him with her bitter explosions. It is said that a pleasant and cheerful disposition aids digestion. Aina apparently had not heard of this.

'I tried to bail you,' Sango said. 'Really, I did, Aina.'

'Marry me, now, Sango. Don't you know I love you very much? Sango, I'll die for you.'

He heard that warning again. The warning voice of his mother, about the women of the city. Letters from her were usually written by a half-literate scribe, but that warning was never in doubt.

'Aina, but —'

'You are very wicked, Amusa.' She was smiling, and that made matters worse, because her smile always melted his heart. 'If someone had told me that you would do this to me, after that night on Molomo Street and the way you said you loved me —'

'We're still friends, Aina.'

CYPRIAN EKWENSI

She was still smiling. He tried to make it easy for her. But how could he make her see that their paths diverged from the very beginning?

'I want to ask you a favour,' she said, as the waiter cleared the table.

Sango lit her cigarette and after she had inhaled deeply, she said: 'I want new clothes: the native Accra dress ... really special. The clothes I had before I went to jail, they're no use to me now. From now on I want to be wearing glamour specs. Nor for my eyes – my eyes are okay – but for fancy. And a gold watch. I have suffered for three months *hard labour*. Now I must enjoy all I dreamed of at night in my cell.'

'But Aina, you know how broke I am, always!' He took out his wallet and found some pound notes which he offered her.

She took them from him without one word of thanks. Nor did she smile. It was then he knew that nothing could alter the bitterness she felt towards him.

Aina regretted not having gone with Sango. She watched his taxi swing into the traffic till it was hidden away by a mammy-wagon. Soon he would be at Lugard Square to see the soap-box orators. Aina looked at her clothes and decided that election time was fashion time, and one way to make certain she would be noticed was to get herself something smart. With only five pounds in the folds of her dress, she had a problem.

On High Street she noticed the sign SALE in large letters on every window of Zamil's shop. Zamil himself was standing knee-deep among the rayons and organdies, the printed cottons and velvets – just the very materials Aina would have loved. He was overwhelmed by customers and so was his sister at the other end of the counter. Dark-haired and pretty in a dark way, she had a large pair of scissors beside her on the counter.

'Suad! Mind the money!' shouted Zamil and fired away

the rest of the sentence in rapid Arabic. Without looking up, Suad continued to zip out the cloth by the yard. There was no one else in this shop but Zamil, his sister, and the customers. It was a family business in which little outside help was employed. Aina glanced round and saw bargains by the dozen. One caught her fancy – a rich plum velvet. She imagined herself wearing a dress of this material, cut by a dressmaker along Jide Street, frilled with lace at the bust-line, around the sleeves . . . the sleeves must be very short, to show off the roundness of her arms. Aina was overcome. It dawned on her that no one was watching.

'Steal it, Aina!' came that irresistible urge. 'They're all looking away!'

She propped herself against the wall. If she took it, she could conceal it in the folds of her dress, sneak out quickly. The customers would still be yelling as they were doing now, Zamil and his sister would still be cutting cloth and piling the pound notes on the counter. Ten yards of material – no more; light enough. . . . Quickly now, before someone comes to buy it! No, they would be too frightened of the price.

Aina moved forward. She stopped. A silence reigned in the shop. She looked up and saw that a man in blue robes with a light blue gilt-edged cap had arrived. Lajide.

'Any more velvet cloth? I want twenty, thirty, forty yards; no fifty yards. Let me see . . . eight wives each one six yards, tha's forty-eight . . . give me fifty yards.'

Everyone in the shop had stopped bargain-hunting. There was a gap of silence, which Zamil immediately tried to fill. 'My sister Suad – she will open a new bale for you. Suad!' And he rattled off in rapid Arabic. Suad left her own customers and came across, smoothing back her rich black hair.

Zamil took a ready reckoner and thumbed through it short-sightedly. 'Twenty-three . . . pounds . . . two an' six, that's the cost of fifty yards.'

'Twenty poun',' said Lajide with confidence, but Zamil

would not give in. The haggling began. The crowd piled nearer the two men.

Lajide sat down, crossed his legs, lit a cigarette. He said: 'Zamil, how you enjoy the new house? Perhaps some of your brothers, they want fine place like that, eh? I got a new house for sale!'

Zamil's manner changed. 'You have a house for sale? I been looking for a house for one of my brothers!'

The daily papers had been featuring long articles about what they called the 'Syrian Invasion', in which they claimed that more and more Syrians and Lebanese were coming into the city and putting the small African trader out of business. They were also depriving him of living accommodation. One of them would take a whole compound and pay the rent demanded five years in advance, while ten Africans would squeeze into one room, musty, squalid and slummy.

'This morning, I got wire from home . . . One of my brothers is also coming. . . . Myself, my sister, and servants in Clifford Street, we're so crowded.'

Lajide laughed. He was obviously one of those unscrupulous men who meant to cash in on the situation. He threw back his head and rocked in a manner that brought a frown to Aina's pretty face.

'The house is not for sale. No! For lease, yes. And is ten thousand. No, we talk about that sometime.'

'Tha's all right for me.'

'There you are! What did I say? You do me good, I do you good.' He regarded Zamil questioningly.

'Pay twenty pounds,' Zamil said, slapping the financier familiarly on the shoulder. 'You are my friend.'

Suad was prompt with scissors and brown paper, and in a few minutes, the full fifty yards were under her brother's arm and he was taking the cloth himself to the jeep and Lajide was having a few final words with him.

Aina did not breathe till she felt the air was freer. She dared not show her face from behind the pillar. She heard the jeep drive away and was almost grateful for what had *not* happened. Suad was shouting about closing time, and already Zamil was half-shutting the doors.

Aina, as she left the shop, was challenged by Zamil who quietly insisted that his sister Suad would search her. It was an embarrassing moment for her when she was led into a private room and stripped to her undergarments. In the folds of her dress Suad found the five pounds Sango had given her.

'Mus' be some mistake,' Zamil apologized later, when Aina rejoined him in the shop. The shop was now quite empty. All doors were closed, except one left open, no doubt for her departure. Zamil was acting queerly, Aina thought.

'But Lajide told me . . . he said . . . are you not the girl who go to jail for shop-lifting.'

'So tha's what you were talking when you went to the car with him, eh?' Aina straightened her cloth. 'Now listen. Lajide is telling lies! You can go and tell him I said so. I work for a Lebanese two years. Baccarat! I never steal one penny in my life. When people don' like you, they can say anything!' Aina gazed steadily into his eyes.

'Most sorry,' Zamil said. 'If I can do anything to help —'

'No! Not you – or Lajide!'

She pushed back the door and was out in the streets. For her it was a proud moment. She wished she could always hold her head as high. She wished she could overcome once and for all that itch to lift things. Then, and only then, would Sango, the man she dearly loved, take her seriously.

Lugard Square was packed to overflowing, and long before Sango had actually arrived at the square he heard the music of First Trumpet floating about the hubbub. He listened for a moment to the hoarse and false promises for better working conditions, improved medical services, more and better houses . . . The speaker was a man from the S.G.N. Party. Many of the audience milled around in groups of their own, some selling cigarettes, many with an eye for a sucker on whom to pull a confidence trick or two. At a bookstall at the entrance to the square Sango bought a copy of the party's booklet for sixpence.

There was no doubt that the S.G.N. Party would win the largest number of seats in the Town Council during the coming election. How the Realization Party was faring Sango found out the same evening. In a narrow lane beside the Methodist church, a man stood on a stool, his features dramatically lit by the dazzling glare of a gas lamp. He was saying much the same thing as the speaker of Lugard Square, namely, more houses, more food, more water and more light for the people.

'He's deceiving us,' said a man on the fringe of his audience. There could not be more than thirty people listening to him.

Sango looked more closely and something in the speaker's manner arrested his attention. It was the kind politician who who offered him a room he would not take. Now, Sango thought, was the time to help him.

After his speech, Sango told him how he had enjoyed his argument, and how he was taken by the R.P.'s ideas. 'You want more listeners. The way to get them is to have some music, some attraction. Let something be going on while you talk.'

'I've tried; I can't get a good band.'

'I'll play for you.'

The politician took off his glasses and looked closely at Sango. 'Young man . . . Oh, it's you! I was wondering where I'd met you! Dele's friend!'

Throughout that week Sango and First Trumpet with the rest of the band toured the streets of the city. Large banners fluttered from their lorry with the words: THE REALIZATION PARTY WILL REALIZE YOUR DREAMS. They stopped at street junctions and one of the representatives would speak to dancing listeners. Very often they wanted to know in advance where the next speech would be.

First Trumpet did not entirely agree with Sango. He thought Sango was a fool not to play for money. But Sango told him: 'We have our weekly engagement with the All Language Club. That will pay for our needs.'

But that Saturday, arriving as usual at eight, Sango heard music coming from the bandstand. He asked for the manager of the Club and was shown into a tiny room by the Club's garden.

The manager seemed to be going through his books. He looked up when Sango knocked and said: 'Ah, Mr. Sango. Sit down!'

Sango felt it coming.

'Now, Mr. Sango; I've engaged the Tropic Rhythms Band to play for me, until you stop this nonsense.'

'I don't understand.'

'For the last five days, you've been playing election music for the Realization Party. I, as manager of this Club, am not in agreement with their policy.'

As he spoke he fingered an envelope lightly. 'I'm paying you fifteen guineas for tonight and fifteen guineas for next Saturday in lieu of notice.'

'But – really, this is ridiculous! I —'

Sango took the envelope and walked across the premises, seeing nothing. First Trumpet joined him.

'Sango, d'you know what I heard? The manager of this Club is broke. He's selling out – and Lajide is to be the new owner!'

'Mere rumour. Don't believe it.'

'It's true. One boy from the Tropic Rhythms told me; it must be true.'

'Okay! Anyway, jus' call the band together, First Trumpet. We've been sacked; so we mus' begin to look for another boss. First let's share our money.'

All this meant some inconvenience. Sango could not think where they would hold their rehearsals from now on. The manager of the All Language Club had been so very kind to them; but now there was no more question of using the club in the afternoons.

Sango was in a blue mood as he walked about the city, drifting with the aimless ones, looking but not seeing. He walked longer and longer into the night because he did not like the thought of going home and also because the lights and the noise created in his guts a restless desire to be part of it.

He hoped that one day he would become editor of the *Sensation*, and settle down with a girl from within this city. But so far, no progress. To him it mattered, for he believed that a man had to have a home behind him if he must build. At the moment, not even the foundations had been laid.

Nothing penetrated his gloom, not even the cruel snort of a bus that nearly ran him over.

'Sango!' It was the voice of a girl.

She was still wearing the same dress she had on when he left her at the Hollywood. 'Where are you going, this night? Better be careful. Some drivers are mad!'

'I'm taking breeze,' said Sango, still startled.

The traffic spun dizzily across where she stood and, when it had calmed down somewhat, she crossed the street to meet him, moving in that way that gave him the greatest pleasure. She linked her hands with his and they walked and talked.

'You look sad. What has happened?'

'Nothing, Aina.'

She was not to be put off. 'When somebody loves you, you do not know, because you are proud. All right! If you like, tell me. If not, I will not worry you.'

He was touched, and he said: 'It won't interest you. There's a place not far from Molomo Street called the All Language Club. You know the place? Well, we used to play there. But now we have been sacked. They gave us our money and told us never to go there again. That's why I'm sad. What I want now is a place where myself and the boys can meet and practise. We can still find work, but we must continue to practise together.'

She smiled. 'Is that all? And you say it won't interest me; but why now?' She puzzled over it for a moment. 'Sango, there's a place on Molomo Street – near your own house. No one uses the place. It is a large compound. In the daytime, the *Alhaji* teaches Muslim children. But in the afternoons, there's nobody there. I can speak to the *Alhaji* for you.'

Aina led the way confidently into a kingdom where Sango felt a complete stranger. He could not believe they were still on Molomo Street till he had gone and sat in the revolving chair in the barber's saloon. Aina left him there and went about her mission.

The barber came limping in, and winked knowingly. 'You take up with her again? I tell you, the girl like you too much.'

Sango smiled. 'Where's Lajide?'

'I see him in his car with that new woman. They say he buy some new place – All Language Club. You know the place?'

'I use to play there, barber.'

Now it was clear. If Lajide had become the lover of Beatrice, it could only mean that she had put the idea of buying the Club into his head.

Aina came back to say that all would be well. The *Alhaji* had given permission. He was very pleased with the idea because he thought Sango's band would make the school popular. Sango and his men could go there twice a week – Mondays and Thursdays – to practise. She smiled happily and said: 'Let us go to the beach by the lagoon and play.'

Again the barber winked, a little more knowingly this time.

Sango had not noticed the moon till he saw the shadows of the coconut fronds waving against the sky. The surf beat with violence and the courting couples were dark clumps on the sands. There was a faint breeze with a tang in it.

'Don't be sad any more,' Aina said, leaning against him.

CYPRIAN EKWENSI

'No more. I'm happy.'

'Because of me? Sango, do you love me now?'

He was silent, trying desperately to collect his thoughts, to marshal his forces against the wiles of this seductress. He looked at her face, serene, with long lashes and pouting lips. In the eyes he read admiration. Just for this once, he decided to be defeated. He held her to himself and she sighed the sigh of love in triumph.

10

Bayo it was who brought the news about the battle for Beatrice. Lajide, as owner of 163B Clifford Street, was at war with Muhammad Zamil, the tenant – or so it seemed. How else could he explain what had happened? Zamil, after buying the house, had allowed Lajide to let one of the rooms to the girl; but he could visit Beatrice only by day. Sleeping in her room was out of the question for a man who had eight wives.

'Tha's where the trouble began,' Bayo said. 'You know that Zamil is a bachelor, always home in the evenings – and Beatrice is the kind of girl that foreigners like.' Bayo glanced round the crowded restaurant where Sango had taken him for lunch and continued: 'I know all this because when Beatrice was there she helped me a lot. I used to meet Suad in her room and no one would know.'

'Wait a minute. "When Beatrice was there," you said just now. You mean – she's no longer there?'

'She left. I don' know where she is now. Perhaps she's gone back home to the Eastern Greens. I heard she was very ill lately.'

'Home is the place for her,' Sango said.

'I wish she had not left Zamil,' Bayo said. 'It has upset all my plans. I've not seen Suad for three weeks now. When I go to the shop I cannot meet her, and at their home it is so difficult.'

He sipped his lime-juice. He had not touched his steak. It was unlike Bayo to show no appetite. 'Sango, what am I to do? I love this girl very much!'

'It will pass away,' Sango said. 'I'm sure it will. She's not taking you seriously. And you are only kidding yourself. Come off it! When that girl meets some young man from her home, you think she'll remember you?'

Bayo sat back in his chair, but his depressed mood remained. Sango could not get him to talk about anything else but Suad Zamil.

Beatrice had become the thorn in Lajide's flesh, the one woman his vanity and money could not conquer in a city where women yielded to money and influence. He could not understand the girl, because their backgrounds were so different. Beatrice came from a poor but proud family where values still mattered. Right was right, but wrong met its punishment. The end was not the most important thing, but the means. Lajide had lived too long in the city to care about right or wrong, so long as the end was achieved. And that end was so often achieved by money that it was inconceivable to him that money could ever fail in anything or with anybody.

Lajide went to see her in the department store. She had told him of her desire to work there and within a week he had made the desire a reality. He boasted to his friends: 'One of the girls in the department store is my gal!'

He saw her now in the top rung of the ladder, fetching down a packet of something for a white woman. She looked ultra-smart in the close-fitting uniform with the 'D.S.' above the breast. Her eyebrows were cleverly pencilled and she wore lipstick.

'Choose one scent – for yourself!' Lajide said impulsively as the white woman made her purchase and left. 'You look too fine, Beatrice!'

'Lajide, please!'

'Ready to close now,' he said possessively.

'Remain half an hour.'

'Beatrice, you vex with me? I go to the restaurant till the time reach.'

'You know that men are not allowed to stand about talking to girls in this store. You must be buying something or moving on. Unless you want me to be sacked?'

'No, no!' he said quickly, and went up into the restaurant above the store.

As he entered, Bayo pinched Sango and said: 'Look! That's Lajide, your former landlord. Let's ask him. Perhaps he has seen Beatrice.'

'Forget it,' said Sango.

Neither of them could imagine the mental torture through which Lajide was passing. The girl was far too stubborn and independent. He was prepared to go any length to make money and yet more money, to consolidate his position with her. It was all strange to him, because he took it for granted that he was master where all women were concerned.

He did not get back home till late in the evening. He was tired. He had a wash, changed into a light cloth, and called Alikatu. She was his third wife. But it was Kekere, Lajide's eighth wife, who came to say that Alikatu was not yet back from the market. She brought him a drink, and curtseying, offered it to him.

Lajide was bored. 'Sit on my knee and amuse me,' he told Kekere.

She was the youngest of them all, about eighteen, with very round eyes. He called her Kekere, which means 'small' because in position she was the most junior of them all. He never did this till he was in a playful mood or wanted some favour from her. Her soft fingers rested on his cheek.

'Why have you been so angry lately? You have neglected all of us . . . Or are we going to be *nine*?'

'Me? Angry? *Nine!* Ha, ha! . . .'

'Where are you going, Kekere?' Lajide said, as she rose laughing from his knee.

'To put on some music.'

'Not too loud! The compound has been very quiet since that Sango left this place. I don't want any noise. My head aches.'

She gave him a saucy look. 'All right! But I'll play my favourite record.'

He watched her bare shoulders. For a girl so young she looked very mature. Her bosom trembled beneath the cloth as she moved. He was excited by the soft freshness of her well-made body.

'Is all right now. Come and sit here.' He tapped his knee.

Beatrice would never obey such commands; and now even Kekere was being naughty. She bent forward and twisted her hips, dancing a wiggle dance to the music. Lajide watched the cloth, fearing it would soon drop off.

'Stop that! I want to think! What'll you say if a stranger enter here and see my wife with her cloth off?'

'No one will come.'

She laughed and continued to tease him with her dance. He was discovering her for the first time. Did he really have a girl like this here, under his own roof and yet —

'Come and sit here, Little One!'

'I hear, my Lord!' She moved, noiseless on her toes, and stood with hands behind her back. 'I'm here.'

'Is this madness?'

She laughed and sat on his knee. He held her close, imagining desperately that she could be Beatrice. He did not see the strangers enter.

Kekere whispered: 'They want you.'

'Who are they?'

'I can see them: two men.'

Lajide had never seen them before, yet they called him by name. Instantly he was on his guard. He pinched Kekere. 'Go into the bedroom. I'm coming . . .'

'So you always say, and you won't come to me. You'll go outside to that woman.'

'Go, I'll meet you. Truly.'

She went. It was not often that love came her way. At the bedroom door, she turned and made eyes.

One of the men carrying a brief-case came into the room.

'We have come to discuss business.' As he spoke his partner entered and they both sat down. 'It is like this. We have five lorries, big, nice, in good condition, We want to sell them, and we want one thousand five hundred pounds for them – spot cash. You can repaint them and sell them at eight hundred pounds each. The timber merchants will grab them quick.' He produced a cigarette and lit it.

Lajide watched him. The directness of the offer left him gasping. He had always thought that no one could excel him in blunt talk. He stroked his chin. Why had they picked on him? On the other hand . . . Beatrice! Here was a chance to spend some real money on her and stun her. That five thousand he had received from Zamil, where was it? Gone . . . he must have some more cash.

'Excuse me gentlemen. Kekere! Kekere! come and get beer for the gentlemen. We can talk better with drinks.'

'Just so, sah!'

Kekere bustled about the inner room. She came out, carrying a tray with bottles and glasses. She set the tray down near them and left. Their eyes followed her.

'You have a very beautiful wife,' the one with the brief-case said.

'And young,' the other added.

'Women are trouble,' said Lajide, thinking about Beatrice. But he could not disguise his pleasure.

'Women soften life. Life is too hard,' said the man with the brief-case.

'Yes; when you have one wife it may be true. But a man like me, I have eight.'

Lajide filled his glass. 'Of course they come and go. Today, six, tomorrow eight. I use to worry myself about them. Not now.' Kekere came out now and wandered about the room. She picked something and slipped back behind the curtains. The men licked their lips.

'Where are these lorries?' Lajide asked.

'Not far from here.'

'What kind of lorries?'

'Very good ones, have no fear. Ex-Army. Used by the Americans and the British during the war. Very good for the timber business.'

While they talked, Lajide kept thinking how he could double-cross these men. The idea did not come all at once. Slowly he rose and went indoors to change.

Kekere lay in bed, half-draped. She looked up. 'Are they gone? Have you come?'

'Pss! Listen! This is what I want you to do. If you bungle things, I won't come to you any more . . .' In a few quick words he gave her his orders and said, 'Now, don't waste time.'

Again and again he warned her that she must do as she was told. Then he went out and met the robbers, who had been waiting impatiently.

It was one of those moonlit nights when a man has to peer into a face to identify it. Lajide approached the men who took him to inspect the lorries. To his amazement he discovered that the lorries were sound: that they needed mere paint – in fact, these men were dealing with him as honestly as one rogue with another. But that did not alter his plan. He too, needed the money and knew well the risk involved.

If Kekere had done her share, the police should be here now. He peered into the darkness, but saw nothing. Then he began to haggle with them, to fill in the time. His ears were tuned for the faintest sounds, and he identified the crunch of boots before anyone else.

A group of men broke into their conversation, two of them in police uniform. Lajide saw the glint of moonlight on handcuffs. The robbers cursed him, but his own men (so he thought) were there awaiting his orders.

'Take these lorries to the Eastern Greens and sell them. You must travel only by night.'

'What are you talking?' asked the uniformed man.

Lajide peered into the face, a strange one and very likely

that of a real policeman. Kekere had bungled his plans. He had instructed her not to summon the real police but his own accomplices disguised as policemen. Kekere's stupidity would cost him thousands of pounds.

He drew back. 'I don't speak to you. Am laughing at the thief-men.'

'You done your duty well,' said the policeman, gleefully. He turned to the lorry thieves and said harshly: 'Inside!' As they clambered into the police van he shook Lajide by the hand. 'Well done!'

Lajide forced a smile and mumbled something but his thoughts were fixed on how best to discipline the frivolous Kekere. When he got home she was nowhere to be found and she did not show up until Providence dealt Lajide a blow.

His third wife, Alikatu, returning from market one evening, had a stroke. By morning there had been a relapse and she lay in a coma – not alive, not dead, not suffering. Lajide was distraught. He dared not leave Alikatu to go and visit Beatrice.

The news spread quickly. The financier's wife was dying. Sango heard it in the *Sensation* office and booked a van to take him to Molomo Street. As he stepped out of the lorry he recognized the leader of the Realization Party who had offered him a free room, rushing round in his siesta jumper and cloth as if trying to shake the sleep from his eyes. From the neighbouring houses women poured into Lajide's compound, pressing their noses against the windows. This whole part of the city seemed to be agitated and anxious as the last moments ticked by in the life of someone they knew and liked.

Sango squeezed through till he could see Alikatu lying on the bed. Her face was pallid. Gone was the radiance that made her one of Lajide's favourite wives. The head wife, fat and busy, pushed him aside and took Alikatu's head in her lap, like a baby's.

She pressed a tumbler to the sick woman's lips. 'Drink it!'

Alikatu gurgled and turned away. 'Drink it,' echoed the

politician. Alikatu gurgled again, spat out the liquid and lay still.

Lajide's head wife looked into the sky with the palms of her hands facing her Creator and called out, '*Olorun-O!*' in this manner offering to God all her prayers for more help and possibly a miracle.

'I think we better fetch a taxi, before is too late!' said the politician. The word taxi was taken up till it was echoed outside. 'Taxi is here!' someone shouted from the streets. An argument arose and in the end the politician said: 'Tell the taxi to go! Is best not to move her. We'll send for a doctor.'

Lajide arrived and saw Sango. 'I don't want you here! Go away. You and that Lebanese thief Zamil, you worry the life out of me. Everywhere I go I see you. Have I no private life?'

The politician held Lajide back, for he was advancing with clenched fists. Sango stood his ground. Tender hands managed to calm Lajide, who sat beside Alikatu and held her head in his arms.

'Alikatu!' he called softly. The feeling he injected into that whispered word, the loving care with which he held his wife, created a restlessness and pain in all present. The man was laying bare his soul before them. He kept glancing behind him expectantly.

Almost on his heels a tall and well-dressed man in European clothes walked into the room and put down his bag. He took out a stethoscope, pressed it to the woman's heart. They watched him in silence. His face betrayed nothing.

He took his bag and went downstairs accompanied by the politician. Sango listened to their whispered conversation. He heard nothing. The doctor continued down the stairs and had hardly gained the street when a wailing cry broke out from the room where Alikatu lay. The story was there – plainly written on every face. But in every face was also engraved that stubborn shade of hope . . . that there might still be just the barest chance . . . that the body lying there – the body of

Alikatu – was not *dead*, only resting. She would still breathe, surely. She would answer when called loudly by name.

A tense crowd hovered in hushed silence along the corridor. Now a man with a black bag – a doctor in the African manner trained by tradition in the ways of the past – this man went down the stairs and began to chalk up the ground and to spatter the blood of a chicken about the house, muttering incantations. He made a great show of the ceremony while the gentle wind blew the feathers about the compound. To Sango it was rather early to begin to frighten off Alikatu's ghost from Twenty Molomo. The herbalist seemed to be giving the final order to the ghost, to be tilting the balance in a particular direction.

'Alikatu!' Everyone knew now. People threw themselves down into convulsions, crying: 'Alikatu!'

The lament in that cry could tear the heart out of a stone. It chilled Sango's blood. As he stood there and listened to the wailing and the moaning, he could also hear the prayers, exhortations, wishes, rebukes, regrets. His soul was stirred. The sobs and sighs shook the frail rafters of Twenty Molomo. Something in the ritual reminded him of the terrible night at Lugard Square, the night of the *Apala* dance. Why, if Alikatu's spirit still hovered around this place, did it not have pity on the poor mortals and re-inhabit the body where it belonged? O, pitiless death.

The mourners came in groups. Sometimes Twenty Molomo was so quiet that one could hardly guess it was inhabited by even a single soul. Then a new and noisy group would come and start the wailing and the moaning and the deafening cries.

What Sango noticed specially was that not one of the people who had been at the festive party at the All Language Club set foot in Lajide's house. They must have heard of his bereavement. Instead they sent flowers. It must be the sophisticated thing to do. They were too busy to come, too busy to hearken to the voice of death which must one day call them one by one.

•   •   •   •   •

Sango went to the 'Waking' because Bayo had promised him there would be lots of girls. A waking in the city was a sad affair, but the living had eyes to the future and many a romance had been kindled in the long-drawn-out hours between night and morning, when resistance is at its minimum and the whole spirit is sympathetic and kindly disposed.

It was no surprise to Sango when, moving among the mourners, the drummers, and those who drank palm wine, he saw Aina. She had indeed bought and tailored her Accra dress and it heightened her charm. Plum velvet it was, bordered with white lace and sewn in the latest style. The blouse showed off the roundness of her arms, and the skirt, a long piece of material artfully tied round the waist, showed off just so much tantalizing thigh, and no more. Sango wondered how the men could keep their minds on death, with Aina so very vibrant with life.

Only one moment before that, Sango had seen Lajide sitting motionless, unaware of the world about him. Lajide's head had been sunk on his breast while Zamil came in briefly to console him. The fact that Lajide had not lifted his head, that he was surrounded by a group of friends who were chosen to prevent him from trying to take his own life, showed Sango the depth of his grief.

The contrast between his attitude and Aina's was clear. Aina had not come to mourn. She was not dressed like the others, in the *aso-ebi*, the prescribed dress of mourning.

She too had seen Sango and she now came towards him, bright-eyed. Some feet away, Sango caught a whiff of her perfume and the dry feeling came immediately to his throat. He desired her immediately. With shame in his eyes he tried to look away, to ignore her presence.

'Hello, Sango, I called at yours several times after that night!'

'Aina, not here! We have come to mourn, not romance!'

'I heard something; is it true that you went home to marry? They said when you went to the Eastern Greens during the crisis you paid the bride-price on your future wife. Is it true she will join you soon?'

Sango smiled. 'Aina! But why are you so angry about it?'

'Don't you know why? It means you have been deceiving me!'

'But did I ever promise to marry you?' He left her abruptly and mingled with the crowd. He wished he could have seen Beatrice, but she was not here, neither was she at the funeral which took place in the afternoon.

Because of the death at Number Twenty, Sango was not allowed to practise with his band at the Muslim School on Molomo Street. The manager of the school, a good friend of Lajide's and a devout Muslim, told Sango that practice was out of the question for a long time to come. There were ceremonies still to be performed at Number Twenty, and again the *Ramadan*, their own festival, was very near and the school premises would be used for rehearsals during the next month or two.

The boys in Sango's band had already begun to disperse to undertake free-lance assignments. Another door had been closed in his face.

II

By polling day all energy had been spent. The politicians were now tired of making promises and had taken their proper places – in the background. Clerks, motor drivers, butchers, market women, shopkeepers, who as responsible citizens had previously registered their names, went to the polling stations that dotted the city, and cast their votes. For that single day, the power was in their hands and the politicians waited with beating hearts and speculating eyes for the results.

It turned out that out of the fifty seats in the Town Council the Self-Government Now Party had won thirty-nine, leaving eleven seats for the Realization Party. This meant that the government was now in the hands of the S.G.N. Party and that they would elect a mayor from one of their leaders.

There had never been a mayor in the West African city and now the first one was to be an African. It was a great triumph for the S.G.N. Party. The *West African Sensation* had been working hard on the elections with such leaders as:

WHO WILL BE MAYOR?
CHOICE OF MAYOR CAUSES SPLIT IN SELF-GOVERNMENT NOW
PARTY
TIME TO REDEEM ELECTION PROMISES
REALIZATION PARTY THROWS BOMBSHELL
NATURAL RULERS AND THE NEW CONSTITUTION

Sango found himself with less and less work to do. Lately he had developed a habit of leaving the office for longer than he should, searching for a place of his own, and a place for his band. Money was the limiting consideration. They were asking for too much, and he had very little.

The crime boys seemed to be taking a rest and the pages of the *Sensation* were losing their spice. McMaster called him into the office and told him to turn his hand to other assignments. There was a shortage of good men and it was a loss to the paper to have a man of Amusa Sango's calibre counting the minutes and doing nothing.

Then the great opportunity came. It was on a morning when the rain had added to his irritations and he had come into the office soaked. He remembered stamping his shoes as he entered the office. Layeni, the night editor, had not left. They were all discussing a subject of national importance.

'A great shock for the nation . . . but anyway, he was an old man . . . Good-bye to the wizard of statesmanship, the inspiration for the new movement . . .'

'Without him, there would be no nationalism today on the West Coast . . .'

Sango knew they were talking about De Pereira, the greatest nationalist of all time. He was eighty-three and though he did not involve himself now in the physical campaigns and speech-makings he was the brains of the S.G.N. Party. For the last twenty years he had been the spiritual leader of the party and the party dramatized his ideals. Sango listened to the idle talk. He did not know as he stood in the *Sensation* office what this would mean in his life. How could he? He was not detailed to cover the item: McMaster selected a special political correspondent. Most offices broke off for the day, and Sango could have gone home if he chose. Instead, he listened.

And as he heard more and more he found what he had missed by not being an active nationalist. The city, the whole country, rose together to pay tribute to De Pereira. Almost within the hour the musicians were singing new songs in his name; merchants were selling cloth with imprints of his inspiriting head. Funeral editions of the *Sensation* featured his life story from the time of Queen Victoria of England to Queen

Elizabeth II, in whose reign he died. They asked the question: in view of De Pereira's death at so critical a time in the history of the S.G.N. Party, who would guide them to ultimate victory for the whole nation? This was too much of a loss for African nationalism. Who else had the experience, the wizardry, the insight, the centuries-old diplomacy of this man who had so long defied death?

During the funeral not a single white man was to be seen in the streets of the city, or anywhere near the Cathedral Church of Christ where his body lay in state. Even those who lived near the Cathedral were shut off by those overflowing crowds that vied for one peep at the magnificent coffin. In the trees above and around the Cathedral people hung like monkeys. Some had even defied the captains of ships anchored in the lagoon and climbed on deck, bravely trespassing, unmoved by the heavy smoke pouring from the funnels.

Sango was seeing a new city – something with a feeling. The madness communicated itself to him, and in the heat of the moment he forgot his worldly inadequacies and threw himself with fervour into the spirit of the moment.

He was one of the suffocated and crumpled men who groaned and gasped to keep alive in the heat and the pressure of bodies half a mile from the Cathedral. He strained to get nearer, and though it was barely two o'clock and the funeral service would not be due for another two hours, he knew he could never get near the coffin.

'Since morning, I stand here!' groaned a man in the crowd. 'I don' know that people plenty like this for this city!'

The heat made time stand still. It was baking hot. It was irritating and unbearable. Two hundred thousand people forming themselves into an immovable block of fiery nationalists who jammed the streets, waiting, hoping to catch one glimpse of the coffin. Death had glorified De Pereira beyond all his dreams.

And Sango was there, more dead than alive, completely stifled by the sweat and squeeze of bodies. He was almost raving mad with irritation. When the wave of movement began from the foot of the Cathedral it came in a slow but powerful wave and beat against the spot where Sango stood. The current reminded him of a river overflowing its banks. Before this pressure the strongest man was flung irresistibly backwards like cork on an angry sea. Amusa staggered, off balance. At the same time he heard a faint cry. A girl in an immaculate white dress was in trouble. She had slipped, and if he did not do something about her that merciless crowd would trample her to death. And she would be the day's sacrifice to the spirit of De Pereira.

He sweated. He tried to disentangle his limbs. The pressure never relented. With his veins almost bursting he managed to bend over, to draw her to her feet. His eyes bulged so much he feared they would burst. His head cracked with pain. He stuck his elbows out so as to receive the surging crowd on a sharper point, shepherded the girl to a lane. Even the lanes were overflowing with people. He managed to push her into a little crevice and then looked at her face. It was tired, but attractive.

She was breathing in short gasps. 'Oh! . . .'

She held her sides. 'I hope you're not hurt,' Sango said quickly. 'Smooth out your dress – they've made a mess of it.'

She leaned against him, bruised and shaken. There was nowhere he could take her to, for all the eating and drinking places had been closed.

'You – you saved my life!'

'Quiet, first. We must still get out of this madness.'

Far down the Marina, by the lagoon, was a little promontory over which the broad leaves of a coconut palm waved. It was quiet and deserted and the wind blew sweet and cool. Sango made her sit down. She looked at him gratefully, not saying a word, and he felt a pain in his heart.

She had unbuttoned her blouse so that the breeze caressed her young body. 'I'll soon be all right,' she said. 'There's going to be an important speech at the graveside.'

'You're not strong enough now, Miss —'

'Beatrice is my name.'

'Beatrice!' A thousand tunes hummed in his brain. 'This is very odd!' He took her hand and now the touch of her hand had a magic enchantment for him.

The fresh air had partly revived her. Slowly they walked for mile after mile, and for Sango it could have gone on for ever without his noticing, so strange was the pleasure which her company gave him and so elated his spirit.

When they caught up with the funeral procession it was still difficult to break through to the front row. And Beatrice the Second – as Sango called her – insisted on remaining till the end. She was indeed showing him what nationalism meant for the people of the city.

'It's like the death of Gandhi,' Sango said. 'De Pereira was, after all, our own Gandhi!'

There had never been anything like this. It was impossible to move one step in any direction. They were obliged to give up and stand about for an hour, rooted to the spot. From somewhere a movement of bodies started. The funeral was over. A new song was born at that moment. It rent the air. Sango, ashamed of his ignorance of the words, could only mumble the most conspicuous word, 'Freedom . . .' which seemed to be the recurrent theme.

'Did you see the coffin?'

'No, but they say it was an expensive one: covered with gold.'

'I thought they said there would be a funeral speech?'

'We'll read it in the papers tomorrow.'

Beatrice the Second was holding a handkerchief to her nose. All about them people were weeping with genuine grief. Sango was disturbed. He felt out of step with the city. A lump rose in his throat and a mist came to his eyes. He turned away in shame, swallowing hard and blinking, embarrassed by a new and softer side of himself.

'Don't cry, Beatrice!' He squeezed her shoulder.

But everybody was crying. Handkerchiefs were going to noses. And the sun was slowly setting on two hundred thousand mourners.

'There must have been something about that graveside speech! It has stirred everyone to lament. Beatrice, let's be going back now. Where do I drop you?'

Sango hailed a taxi. His conscience troubled him, as he thought: *You have no home, Sango; you have no money; your goods are still at the railway station; you want all the money you can put aside for that six months' rent in advance.* He ignored his misgivings. Nothing must spoil the beauty of this moment. He tried to think of something to say, but no words could express how he felt. His response to this girl made him feel they had been friends all his life. He held her hand.

It was a slow drive through the chaotic city. Sango was irritated by the closeness and the dust, but he was pleased because he could talk to Beatrice the Second and get to know her. She was quite frank about herself.

'I have a fiancé in England. He's a medical student in his third year. I love him very much.'

The words hurt Sango.

'I'll join him soon,' she said. 'I'll do nursing and midwifery. And when we return, we'll have our own hospital in the remote interior. No city life for us! I think they have quite enough hospitals and medical attention here. We'll go to the bush, where we are needed.'

'Good idea,' Sango said. 'But you'll not make much money.'

'I agree. But that's not all there is to it. We will be doing something, giving something . . .' As she talked, she brightened. A new glow came to her cheeks. Her eyes danced. She became a new girl. Sango was full of admiration.

'The city is overcrowded, and I'm one of the people overcrowding it,' Sango said. 'If I had your idea, I would leave the city; but it holds me. I'm only a musician, and a bad one at that. A hack writer, smearing the pages of the *Sensation* with blood and grime.' He saw the interested way in which she leaned forward when he talked about himself.

Lights shone in the streets and long cars began to steal effortlessly through the night, freed at last from the traffic restrictions. The city was gradually recovering from its shock, exerting its everlasting magic.

'I wish I could see you again!'

Sango saw her hesitation. 'I'm grateful to you. I'll tell my father all you did for me . . .'

'I'm sorry, I have no address at the moment, except Crime Reporter, *West African Sensation*. I used to play at the All Language Club, but that road is now closed.'

The taxi pulled up before an old-type house, probably Brazilian. Beatrice the Second stepped gingerly down. She was much recovered now, and the shock was gone.

'I'll see you again,' she said. He took her hand and squeezed it.

He watched her walk away and there was a sadness in his heart. *There is the girl for you, Sango. If you could win her, you would find a foothold in this city and all your desires would focus on a new inspiration. How different she is from them all: Aina, Elina, Beatrice the First. Have you ever felt anything like this beautiful feeling before? But it's hopeless. She herself told you she is engaged and loves her fiancé.*

Sango thought of Beatrice the Second as he sat down in the *Sensation* office to write his report. His despondency filtered into the general tone of his account of the De Pereira funeral. He was poring over the typewriter, a cigarette dangling from his mouth, when he heard footsteps in the corridor. McMaster poked his head into the room and said to Sango:

'A moment, please!'

The telephone was ringing as McMaster entered his office. All the *Sensation* telephones had been ringing incessantly throughout the day. McMaster had the telephone in his hand when Sango entered and with one hand he waved him into a seat.

Sango wondered what it was all about.

'I've had my eyes on your work for some time,' said McMaster when the conversation was over. 'The coal crisis, the Lajide funeral, the election campaigns, and so on. But with the De Pereira affair, I think we're set for your most important achievement. I've had it hinted that you might be offered the post of Associate Editor, depending what the Board of Governors thinks . . .'

Sango went deaf. He opened his lips and no words came.

'Of course, it may be that you prefer the adventure of reporting. This will be an office-chair job. You may like to go and think the whole thing over . . .'

He was still sitting there after the conversation, and one thought was uppermost in his mind: Beatrice the Second. He was becoming a man, fit for a girl of her class. Beatrice the Second . . .

'All right now, Sango.'

Lajide had not gone to the De Pereira funeral. He was alone; probably the only living being on Molomo Street. But his wives had gone. Nothing could keep them indoors these days. He lifted the glass to his lips, made a face, belched. Lately he had developed a habit of talking aloud to himself: 'Since my wife died, everything has changed. Everything! Beatrice – she has no ear for my words. Kekere – she goes out openly to the street lamp on the corner. There she talks to young men. She thinks I do not see her. Ha, ha! Young men on bicycles! She must think I'm a fool. I know all, I see all; only, I don't talk!'

He drank more. That was another new development. The law called this liquor illicit gin, because it was distilled without licence. But the brewers who lived in timber shacks by the lagoon, they called it O.H.M.S. in honour of the Queen of England. The irony of it! Breaking the law to honour the Queen! Of course, they did not let the liquor mature like genuine distillers; that would take too long. But it was still alcohol. If you were not prejudiced you would not be able to distinguish the taste from that of pure gin.

He tossed the glass aside. No good would come of too much thinking. Alikatu – she was dead and gone. The five thousand from Muhamad Zamil was gone and he had not lived at 163B for three months yet. And this new four thousand from the timber deal? When you were in a prominent position and you lost your wife, four thousand pounds *might* see you through all the ceremonies and sacrifices – if you were the showy type like Lajide.

'I must do something . . . I must do something. . . .'

The timber business? He had tried that. He was still on the list of the city's exporters of logs. Everybody was timber-crazy and he might as well take his chance.

His gaze focused suddenly on the door. A strange woman was standing there, in a big-sleeved blouse, a velvet cloth about her waist. No, it could not be Alikatu. Alikatu was dead. Alikatu was dead . . . dead. She would not wear her cloth the wrong way round . . . She always dressed correctly. *Alikatu!* He stood up and reached for her. She was smiling.

'Alikatu!' His throat worked and his eyes bulged. She was smiling defiantly. She was beyond his reach. 'What are you saying? Your lips are moving. I cannot hear you. I cannot hear — No! Not yet . . . I'll join you when my time here is up. Truly, I'll come . . . You have always been my favourite wife . . . I'll come, in *Olorun's* name, I will . . .'

She was no longer standing there, but instead Kekere was at the door and saying something. 'I thought I heard you talking . . . Who was it? Who was it?'

Lajide crept back to his seat, not speaking. One by one his other wives were coming into the room, rigged and preened like courting birds. They were coming from the crowd, from the city and its noise.

'What's wrong, Kekere, tell us. You were here with him!'

'No, I've just returned. I came in. As I was coming in, I thought I heard somebody talking.'

They looked at her suspiciously. She was the youngest of them all and completely frivolous. In her low-cut blouse, which showed far too much of her firm breasts, she seemed capable of anything.

'Truly,' she said. 'I'm not lying. When I came in, I – I thought he was looking at – at me. I was standing there, at the door. And I asked him whether he was talking to somebody and he did not answer.'

'If you have done nothing to him, why does he look so queer? Better speak the truth now!'

'Lord receive my soul!' Kekere swore, noisily slapping her skirt. 'Me? What could I possibly do to him?'

The six women sensed a mystery. Of course no one mentioned the word poison. Where each woman sought the husband's affection, a love potion might be given with good intentions.

Soft hands found the husband's armpits . . . wrapped round his knees . . . around his waist . . . Sweet breaths were indrawn and the aroma of delicate perfume filled the air . . . and as feminine silk rustled, the seven wives, now burdened with the snoring husband, bore him as lightly as they might into the bedroom.

'You'd all better go and change your clothes,' said the fat woman, the Number One wife, taking charge. 'I'll watch over him.'

12

'It's all my fault,' Bayo said. He trudged beside Sango on their way to the left luggage shed where Sango's things were kept. He was in such a state that he followed Sango wherever he went, trying to get a word in about his love affair. 'Sango, the girl Suad warned me all the time to be quick and marry her. She warned me. Truly, she did; but I was unable to marry her. No money. I kept postponing. And now, Sango. Can you believe it? What she said is coming true! Her brother wants to fly her back to Syria. But is that really possible? Just because the poor girl is in love with me?'

'When is the flight?'

'On Monday! Today is Saturday. What can I do? Too late! Oh Lord. My dear, loving Suad Zamil. She has cried so much! Her brother said he'd disown her if she so much as mentions my name again in his ears. She doesn't care. Goes on calling Bayo, all the time.'

Sango found his box and now fumbling for his keys, opened it and began to remove an old script. He took out the clothes he wanted and together they went to a gents' near by to change.

'Sango, you mean this is where you actually keep your things? You haven't found a place? Of course the room of First Trumpet is too small to contain both your things. But this is awful. I'm very sorry. Where do you practise with your band? How can a man live like this?'

Sango said not a word. He was gradually changing his clothes, and Bayo was still talking. 'They're keeping her away from me. Muhamad Zamil is watching over her with a loaded revolver. He doesn't let her out of his sight. Beatrice is no longer there. If she had been there, I could have some excuse of visiting the place. I'm very worried, Sango.'

'How did this matter leak out in the first place?'

'I can't tell you the whole story, Sango. But I suspect Beatrice has something to do with it. You remember Zamil took her to "wife". Well, jealousy can do a lot, you know. And revenge too. You see, it was Beatrice who introduced Suad Zamil to me and we fell in love. She became jealous because the girl liked me at once. Of course we used to meet in her room and she was kind to us. But I never once suspected she would betray us. You see, she and Suad quarrelled. Suad did not like the idea of her brother merely keeping an African woman, and yet *she* was in love with me! I can't understand it all, Sango. It's complicated. But anyway, Zamil knows now, and is guarding her. This thing has gone to high quarters.' Bayo wrung his hands.

'Have you been to the Welfare Office? Tell them you want to marry the girl; that the girl is old enough to decide things for herself, but her guardian will not let her do her will.'

'I've been there!' Bayo said furiously. 'Red tape was against me. They even said they were closing for the holidays. By the time they re-open the girl would be safely home!' He flung his cigarette-butt on to the lavatory floor. That gesture of despair touched Sango. A man came in and they went out on to the station platform. Idly, Sango and Bayo watched a shunting engine. When you lived near a railway station the noise of the engines ceased to sound in your ears.

'Why not go away on a train?' Sango suggested. 'Take the girl and run away. It's romantic! Don't laugh, people do it. At least, you'll leave Zamil alone to look after his shop; and when he cools off, you come back. After all, the girl has her own life to lead. And if you're the man she's chosen, you must see she is happy.'

Bayo's condition was pitiful to see. Dull were his shoes, wrinkled his tie; and the hair of this erstwhile dapper youngster was for once uncombed. Was this the same Bayo who trifled with women's hearts? So terrified of everything that might hurt Suad Zamil? Bayo who was usually so confident in such affairs?

'Just think of Zamil,' he went on bitterly. 'How many girls does he "marry" in a year? I know of Beatrice. Now he's taken another – a half-caste called Sybil. But she's not so new; they were "husband" and "wife" long before he met Beatrice. She has two daughters for him. Zamil makes Suad unhappy by all this and she wants him to settle down. He pays the girls good money if they are virgins. Then he throws them away after his curiosity has been satisfied. What future have girls like Sybil and Beatrice? What decent man will ever take them into their own homes and keep them? Yet, just think! It is this same Zamil who must hold Suad from me! It is he who must guard her morals . . .'

'When last did you see Suad?'

'Before I went to that waking . . . you remember? When Lajide's wife died.'

'That's about two months ago. How then has this thing suddenly flared up? Okay, Bayo! If they're taking her away from you, we must make one last effort to see her. We're going there – this night, Bayo!'

'She told me to get a special licence. I went to the magistrate and he insisted on seeing her in person. There can be no marriage without a bride, or someone to give the bride away! One thing, Sango! I do not want to make this girl suffer for my sake. I love her too much. Please do not come with me tonight. It's too dangerous for two people.'

'I'll come, Bayo. I want to see this girl Suad. Do you realize I've heard so much about her, yet do not know the future bride of my best friend?'

They walked on through the city, wrapped in this problem. Round and round they talked on the same topic: how wrong-doing is a hill, and how one mounts this hill and descries that of another: Zamil and Suad, Bayo and Beatrice, Sango and Aina. . . . And as Sango kept his eyes open for the notice ROOM TO LET, he was thinking how different life would soon be. Associate Editor, *West African Sensation*: but then he remembered the way Beatrice the Second had said 'I have a fiancé in England . . . I love him very much'.

He began to walk faster.

A little after midnight, two figures crept into the garden at 163B Clifford Street West. Lights were still on in the main building. From one of the rooms, the radio was blaring forth Arabian music.

'Which one is her room, Bayo?'

'We can't get in . . . it's at the back.'

'We'll try. I have a little plan. This is all the money I've been saving for that new room: just ten pounds. I'll give some to the night watch. That'll put him on our side. After all, how much does he earn in one month?'

He disappeared. Bayo stood looking at Suad's window. It was in darkness. She couldn't have fallen asleep. She must be as troubled as he was. Just two nights more in the city, then she would embark on that forced journey back home – to what? A dull life, at best. Her love, her life was here in the land where her brother had been all but naturalized. But would she be ready to elope with him now? The reckless thought frightened him.

Sango came back. 'She's sitting in the lounge. Bayo, she's a beauty! She's worth any sacrifice! But that fool Zamil is there too. And a strange woman – perhaps the Sybil you told me about. Some children too. No one seems to go to bed in this house. Wonder what we can do. This is a little harder than I expected.'

They crept into the yard. The steward was drying his hands on a napkin. He took Bayo aside and for a long time they argued and sighed – in whispers. Then the steward took a trayful of glasses into the large house. 'Zamil is drunk. We may be lucky. I'll try for you, if it can be possible.'

They waited. Soon he was back. 'I have made signs to Suad. Is best for you to wait her in the cotton bush, behind the window. No one will see you there.'

Bayo went there and waited. Amusa went back to the night watch. Time crawled. He tried to imagine how the girl would be feeling now. Then he heard a rustle, delicate and light. A white figure in a pink dressing-gown flitted by. He saw the eagerness with which the two lovers embraced each other. Sango looked away with a sigh of pleasure. This alone, this abandon was enough reward for their effort.

Suad lifted her face to be kissed. She was breathing with some pain as if the tears choked her throat. 'The licence? You have got it?'

'They said you must come. And two witnesses.'

'What we can do? I fly in two days. My brother, he has made all the arrangements. This night, tomorrow night, that's all! Oh! I don't want to leave you, my Bayo! My African love!' She took his face between her hands with all the tenderness of a mother fondling a baby.

'Do you love me, Bayo?'

'I cannot sleep because of you.'

'I love you too much. Bayo, kiss me!'

Bayo took her in his arms and kissed her with all the hunger of repressed love. Her lips were warm in their mad response.

'Bayo!' she whispered.

They were silent, treasuring the precious moments of their love. She it was who said, 'Bayo, maybe we can run away! Yes, we can, my love!'

'Can you come – now? No, Suad! Do not come. It will be too much suffering for you. And —'

'I have some money. We can run away and never return. Never, never! Then Zamil will suffer.'

'Enough talk! You are afraid, no?'

'I'm not afraid.' He could not bear to see her dejection. 'Suad, I'll die for you! In the whole world there's no girl like you, Suad,' he said impulsively. 'Go and get your clothes.'

He was very muddled about it all, but there was no way out now, only forward. 'Go get your things.'

At that moment the steward appeared. 'Missus. I don' know what's wrong with Master. He's searching everywhere for you.'

'You haven't seen us, steward. Understand?'

'Suad!' came the harsh call. 'Suad!' It was Zamil.

Suad nestled quickly in Bayo's arms, wringing from their brief meeting all the joys of persecuted young love. His fingers sought her soft hair. Her frenzied lips searched fervently, not merely for his lips, but for his soul, probing for signs of assurance . . . searching for the slightest hint of fear or lack of constancy. 'Good-bye, Bayo, kiss me, my love, and let me die.'

'No, Suad. We go together. Without you, I die. Pack your things, let's escape.'

'Bayo, it is impossible. Embrace me, sweetheart, before I die.'

'Hands off!' Zamil had emerged from the bushes, dishevelled wild. In his fist a dark object rested.

'Muhamad, don't be silly. Put that gun away.'

A shudder ran through Bayo. 'Keep still, Suad.' His body vibrated with a new surge of joy and courage. 'Your brother is a coward, and will do nothing. He's strong only with a gun. Here, let me have the gun.'

'Where are you going? Bayo, be careful. He's drunk —'

Zamil stood his ground, but Bayo leapt. Two cracks split the air.

Bayo groaned, clutching his stomach. Suad screamed. This was the final moment. The life was ebbing fast from him. The warmth glowed upwards but down below all feeling drained and faces of evil menace, void and empty, ricocheted with the night in a kaleidoscope of grimaces. Death had ceased to be a stranger. Suad clung to him, and lifeless and tangled together both of them crashed to earth.

The gun dropped with a clatter. Zamil's eyes had become

clear as drinking water. His madness had vanished with the slaughter of the two lovers who were too happy to know or care.

Sango had seen and heard the shooting. Desperately he hoped that no great harm had been done. He clutched his stomach, resolutely trying not to be sick, but up it came. He could not help it. There was a tap near by, and when he had soaked his head and rinsed his mouth Sango felt a little better. When he got up he went to the public telephone and made a call to the police.

The speed with which their van arrived surprised him. Yet Zamil was nowhere to be seen. His car had vanished from the garage. The Inspector waited patiently, convinced by the bloodstains in the cotton bush and the deep marks on the floor where the bodies had apparently been dragged that there *had* been a killing here.

'Is it not the same Zamil of the counterfeit case? The one who was apprehended near Magamu Bush some time ago.' The inspector was surveying the garden, flashing his torch-beam on every blade of grass. 'We've had our eyes on him for some time. He hasn't escaped us this time. We'll get him!'

On Clifford Street West the loco workers who had a morning shift at 6.30 had begun to assemble. By dawn 163B Clifford Street West was the focus of the city's speculations. A love crime! Still Zamil did not show up. Even the steward had vanished.

By 10 a.m. a call came through. It was from the Emergency Ward of the General Hospital, and the inspector recognized the voice as belonging to one of his colleagues. A man had just been admitted with severe head injuries. It was suspected that he had tried to take his own life by shooting himself. He had been found about five miles away at Elizabeth Beach, lying unconscious in his own car. The fisherman who saw him had taken him by canoe across the lagoon to the General Hospital.

'Describe him!' said the inspector, drawing Sango near the receiver so that he too might hear.

The description tallied with what Zamil would look like with severe head inquiries. But the inspector would not take the hospital's word for it.

'I'll be right over,' the inspector said.

And Sango went with him. This will be my greatest story, he thought, as they got into the police van.

'I'm sorry to have to take so drastic a step, Sango,' said McMaster. He was being very much the editorial adviser, Sango's boss sitting in the editorial chair in the offices of the *West African Sensation*. He was not the friend that Sango had worked with for two years. 'You understand how it is – a matter of policy. The *Sensation* does not stand for playing one section of the community against the other. Personally I have nothing against you or your writing in this tragic affair. . . . But I do not own the *Sensation* —'

Sango fingered the letter of dismissal. He was not really listening to McMaster. He was thinking in confused circles: Beatrice the Second, First Trumpet, Lajide, Twenty Molomo; and back to that terrible midnight, small-hours shooting. His rage and disgust; his oath of vengeance. It had now worked in reverse. He had been fired.

'Amusa, less than a week ago, I thought we were all set for something really big: something you deserved. I'd always wanted you to take over the editorship when the need arose; with your drive, your fluent style of writing, your initiative —'

'Must we go over it all again? You've paid me off, you've given me a decent testimonial —'

'Personally I have nothing against you, Sango. Look, I don't often go into details in matters of this kind. But I feel I owe you an explanation for purely personal reasons. You're a good journalist – perhaps the most original in the city. All your writing invariably presents a fresh viewpoint. But in your handling of the Zamil murder case, you seemed to overreach yourself. You made an issue of it, and not a very satisfying one at that. Bayo fell in love with Suad Zamil. Right! The brother, Muhamad Zamil, objected, wanted to fly the girl out of the country. Bayo decides to elope with the girl. Zamil, drunk, shoots Bayo, wounds the girl who later dies in hospital. Zamil runs away, and is later found lying on the beach with bullet wounds in his head. That's your story-line . . .'

Sango smiled. 'As far as you were concerned, that was my story-line. But don't forget, Bayo was my personal friend. And I was present when Zamil shot and killed him, and the girl he loved. The least I could do —'

'Was to fight him in the Press?' McMaster flicked away an ash.

'Naturally.'

'I see . . . Now it's a little clearer why you let yourself go to the extent you did. I'm not sure it was the best way you could have won public sympathy. But I know how it feels to have your best friend killed right before your eyes. It happened to me in France during World War One. Well, you've won your fight. Zamil will die of his wounds; or if not, he'll be hanged. But your reports were most embarrassing. The Board of Governors employed all tact and influence to avoid legal action. As you know we have never been popular either with the *Daily Challenge* or the *Daily Prospect* who regard us disdainfully as the voice of the British Government. A fine mess we're getting into!'

There was little more to be said. As Sango walked down the steps, he heard Layeni saying loudly to the others: 'Yes! . . . These rude college boys! They have no respect for their seniors! Imagine writing things like that for all to read! I've been with the *West African Sensation* fifteen years yet I wouldn't dare . . .'

Sango stepped quickly into the street, tearing himself from the people and the place to which he had become attached. On the lagoon a fisherman was taking advantage of a break in the rains to dry his nets. Beatrice the Second! He had begun to plan how they would both benefit from his new promotion; and now . . .

13

Sango was sitting under his favourite coconut palm by the lagoon looking at the ships and cargo vessels. It was a busy afternoon. Down the road came lorries from the hinterland, loaded with produce to be stacked in the adjoining warehouses. It was the usual afternoon scene on this part of the lagoon and Sango caught himself dozing in the still, oppressive air. Looking up for a brief moment he saw a lorry careering down the road. Something about this particular lorry caught his attention.

It could be the sign, painted in yellow letters on a black background: TRAVEL TO GOLD COAST OVERLAND. Or the numerous flags which fluttered from all parts of the lorry. But the real fact was that it was completely out of tune with its surroundings.

'Amusa! Amusa Sango!' came the sharp cry of a female voice, and at that moment the lorry pulled to one side.

Sango could see no one. From the lorry, a short and stocky man came down, followed by a girl whom Sango immediately recognized as Beatrice the First.

'She recognized you first,' said the stocky man.

Beatrice was smiling. A large raffia hat shielded her head and shoulders from the sun and through her dark goggles Sango could not see her eyes. Yet it seemed to him then that something had gone out of Beatrice the First. This could not be the same girl who had set his blood aflame in those nights when his band had pride of place at the All Language Club.

'Sango, this is Kofi. He's a transport owner who travels between here and Accra.'

Kofi extended his hand. 'I've heard so much about you. I feel I actually know you.'

Beatrice linked her hands with Kofi, and Sango thought: So now it's Kofi. Happiness at last. You will now forget Zamil and Lajide.

She was pale and very thin and when she coughed Sango could not bear the sound.

'Beatrice has been ill and is only just recovering.'

'I'm all right,' said Beatrice brightly. 'Sango, I went to look for you at the All Language Club.'

'You know I don't play there any longer. Not since the manager sold it to Lajide.'

'I was hoping to call at the offices of the *West African Sensation*.'

'You wouldn't find me there, either. Lost my job. Fired. Just this morning. It's a fine day, isn't it? A fine day to lose one's job.'

'I'm sorry, Sango.'

'Beatrice is a very good girl,' Kofi said. 'She's been with me for a little while, and we've been happy. Not so, Beatrice?'

'Yes, and you've furnished our flat wonderfully. Kofi, don't forget, you will drop me near Lajide's house . . . I want to see him alone. Perhaps Sango is coming our way – or is he too busy?'

'I'll come,' said Sango.

They drove through the streets till they came to the turning where Beatrice would get down. Kofi got out to help her down.

'D'you want me to come with you?'

'No, Kofi. I shan't be long.'

She kissed him on the cheek and as she walked down the street, Sango sighed. She could still be the heart-snatching Beatrice he used to know.

'She's a funny girl,' said Kofi tenderly. 'I have never

understood her and never shall.' He stood still until Beatrice turned the corner.

Kofi climbed back into the lorry. 'D'you mind coming to my place? We live on the outskirts of the city. You'll like it. We can have a drink, and talk about you, and —'

'Beatrice!' Amusa laughed. He liked Kofi and in a way was sorry for him. That dog-like attachment to Beatrice!

'I'll tell you something: a moment ago, you said you lost your job. I think you need a holiday. Why not come to the Gold Coast? It will be a real change for you.'

'The Gold Coast? But I don't know anyone there.'

Kofi laughed and turned on the engine. The lorry responded with a throaty rhythm. 'You know me. Look! We will talk about it a little more.' The lorry was moving through the streets. 'My lorries run to the Gold Coast every week. Whenever you want to go, let me know. Here is my card. We are going to my house now, and you will know where we live.'

The idea was appealing. Sango thought the Gold Coast would be a good place for a honeymoon. He took the card and slipped it into his pocket.

Lajide, draped loosely in a floral cloth – his own version of a pyjama suit – walked into the sitting-room to find Beatrice already seated. A full row of his seven wives occupied the divan on the other side of the room. He waved an impatient hand at them.

'What are you all doing here? Get out and let me speak to my visitor!'

He drew a chair and said: 'Welcome, Beatrice.'

She fanned her face with the straw hat. 'I have come to see you about Sango. I've just seen him and he told me he would like to play for the All Language Club —'

'I don't want to hear anything about Sango. I thought there was something else . . .'

Beatrice hesitated. 'There *was* something else . . .'

Lajide looked up. 'What?'

She opened her handbag, took out a bundle of papers. For three days she had been carrying these papers. 'Do you know Messrs Tade and Burkle?'

'Timber dealers? Yes, I know them.'

'They're planning to put you to court.' He looked surprised, and she added: 'They say you altered the marks on some timber they sold to an American firm —'

'Ah! But I bought the timber from them . . .'

'You have altered the marks and put your own marks.' She waved the papers. 'These are the real receipts of the actual buyers.'

Lajide smiled. 'You got those from Tade and Burkle. Never mind. Let them put me to court. I have my own receipts too. Two hundred tons of timber at twenty-five pounds a ton. Is that all, Beatrice? Thank you. You have done well. I was annoyed with you at first for leaving me because of that transport lorry-driver. Yes, I know all about that. I have seen you in his lorry. But now, I see that it's me you love. Beatrice, won't you come back to me? I'll treat you well this time. That timber man is not better than I am.'

Beatrice smiled. 'Money is not everything. A man can have money and still not be a gentleman.'

'I am a gentleman! More gentleman than Sango or the lorry-driver.'

'You're mistaken. No gentleman calls himself by the name. Let people see your deeds and judge.'

'Beatrice, you drive me to hell! I don't know what I see in you. With my position, and all my wives! What you're doing to me, is it good, Beatrice?'

She rose. 'I must be going home now.'

'Back to that man?'

'I just heard about Tade and Burkle and I thought to come and warn you. I don't want you to go to jail.'

He moved near and held her hand. He must have caught a whiff of her perfume, for he tried to press his attentions on her.

'Not here, Lajide! Take your hands off! Now look what you've done to my clothes!'

She went to the long mirror and straightened her dress. 'I'm going, Lajide. Good-bye!'

One thing she knew. Lajide would never be able to find those receipts. The fact was that Tade and Burkle had made a silly mistake. They had sold the mahogany logs to Lajide at a ridiculous price, only to discover that an American dealer was paying much better money for them. To protect themselves they had to recover Lajide's receipt, and to Beatrice had been assigned the task. Beatrice had been able to obtain the receipt from Lajide's clerk, but for days she could not get herself to take them to Messrs Tade and Burkle because she still felt a sense of loyalty to the financier. She decided to give him one last chance. If he would compromise on the Amusa Sango situation, she would not betray him.

On her way down the steps she paused at Sango's old room, then with firmer steps she walked into the street.

Beatrice was waiting for her taxi under the almond tree when the seven women made straight for her. She saw them coming but could not run for it. They beat her with fists, tore her clothes, scratched her skin till the paint and powder ran with blood and sweat. All the concentrated venom and fury, all the hatred which her open intrusion into their household had awakened – she had it all back in that devastating free-for-all.

'Come and see Lajide's mistress!' The cry was taken up all along Molomo Street, and in some ways it reminded them of the cries of 'Thief! Thief!' that had greeted Aina when she emerged from Amusa Sango's room.

Beatrice screamed for help, but no help came. She fell to her knees and no one raised her. Kekere arrived, carrying a bowl. She dipped her hands into the contents and viciously rubbed them over Beatrice's eyes. Cayenne pepper! While the other wives held Beatrice down, Kekere rubbed the pepper into her nostrils, mouth, and – on an impulse – into her most private parts. Then and only then did they leave her to writhe and wriggle in shame and humiliation, disgraced, deprived of every vestige of attractiveness that had led their lord and master astray from them. She had received the treatment normally due to 'the other woman'.

When Lajide heard news of the beating-up he was angry, then miserable. He could not openly declare his support for Beatrice. In some ways he felt she had got her due. But he still loved her. Over and over again, he exclaimed: '*Women!*' with such an accent that those who knew all the facts felt sorry for him. He went into his bedroom, away from it all.

Somewhere in the compound of Twenty Molomo Street, his wives were chanting and wiggling their hips in triumph.

14

The invitation from Beatrice the Second was at least two weeks old. It had missed its way all round the world and finally found Sango.

'I shall dress up and just go; that's what I'll do,' Sango murmured while knotting his tie.

His coat lay on the table beside the invitation. He had almost forgotten how nice it felt to be neatly dressed and to smell of talcum powder.

'Amusa, are you in?'

The question was followed by a knock and Aina came into the room.

'Aina! Who showed you my place?'

'You don't worry about me, so I say let me come and find you.' She was enjoying his embarrassment.

'Very kind of you.'

She sat down without being asked, familiarly, possessively. 'Since I came out of prison, you don't care to send me anything.'

'Like what?' Sango asked, straightening his tie.

'Twenty years is not for ever, Amusa. I have come out of jail. I didn't die there —'

'Come to the point, Aina. You always go round and round. Always. When you want paper for wrapping, you go round. When —'

'I want you to help me because . . . I am pregnant!'

'*What!*' All the drowsiness vanished from his eyes. Even First Trumpet got out of bed and opened the window. The bed was too narrow for one, but it was the only one in the room and he and Sango used it in turn. When they returned in the early hours of the morning after an all-night vigil at some den, they cared for little else than to crawl in there and remain till morning. This evening, Sango was sacrificing his usual all-night stand for the pleasure of Beatrice's company. He looked at Aina and said: 'So you're pregnant. And you think I am the father —'

'Since *that night* at the beach, I have not been feeling well. I didn't want to come till I was sure.'

'Enough!'

Sango did not wish to be reminded of that night when he had walked with her in the moonlight, when she had tried to be kind to him because his band had nowhere to go for practice.

'My mother is prepared to take you to court to claim damages if you refuse to marry me.' She kept her eyes on him and smiled. 'Perhaps you'll let us have about ten pounds to maintain ourselves till the child is born.'

'At a time like this! And you have the guts to smile. Oh, what a fool I've been!'

'But everybody knows you're my lover, Amusa; it's only you that keep making a fuss. What's in it, after all?'

'So every time I raise my head in the world, every time I collect a few hard-earned pounds, you, Aina, come and stand in my way – with a new misfortune! Look, do you know this is blackmail? I could take you to the police – they know your record.'

'I'm not afraid of them. What do I care?'

Which was not the same for Sango. He cared for Beatrice the Second – so much that she must not sully her ears with this nonsense. And there was his mother to think of. He had heard nothing as yet from her. This was a bad situation, whichever way he looked at it. There was no way out.

'I'll give you what I can now, Aina. And I beg you to keep

away from me – for good! The baby cannot be mine, and you know it! I'm helping you because . . . well, because of memories!'

She took the money – all he had saved – and First Trumpet turned as she was leaving.

'What are you going to do, Sango?'

'The child is not mine! Certainly not, and she knows it. If that girl continues to pester me, I shall . . .'

'Kill her? Then you'll hang. For such an irresponsible creature, too! The law doesn't ask about that. At the same time, you cannot afford a second scandal. Your mother, for instance: have you thought of her?'

'But I have no more money! Something must be done. I know she'll come again. Someone is behind this scheme!'

'We've got to think it over,' said First Trumpet. 'You'd better hurry. You're getting late for your appointment.'

Sango thought First Trumpet sounded as if he himself were personally affected. He was a good friend.

'Ah – Mr Sango,' said a grey-haired old man, rising. He was very much a part of the Brazilian-type house, one of the legacies of the early Portuguese invasion of the city. His hand-clasp was crushing for one of his age. Over his shoulder Sango could see large framed diplomas that proclaimed his member-ship of the *Ufemfe* society. 'Sit down and make yourself at home. Beatrice and her mother will soon be here.'

Sango walked on the welcoming carpets with some gravity. This was no rent-grabbing type of house but a real home. He felt uneasy in his stiff collar and bow tie. There was too much starch in his white coat so that it creaked like a rusty door every time he craned his neck to speak to Beatrice's father. He envied the man in his bright robes and handsome necklet of beads.

'I've been anxious to make your acquaintance since that day when you saved my daughter's life. She speaks highly of you.'

Sango smiled. 'She's a wonderful girl; I've never met anybody like her.'

A servant entered, bearing a bowl of kola nuts. He set this down on the little table on which stood decanters and all kinds of drinks.

'Yes,' said the old man, offering Sango a nut. 'She's a wonderful girl! Just like her two sisters – they're married now. One married an engineer and the other a lawyer. Beatrice is the youngest and we dote on her. Yes, we do. But we can't keep her too long. Her fiancé, who is studying medicine at Edinburgh, is pressing for her to join him. It will break our hearts to lose her.'

No words could have torn Sango's heart into more painful shreds. He lost all hope of ever winning Beatrice. He cursed himself for ever having linked his ambitions with hers.

Beatrice's mother had a beaming countenance that spelt happiness. She was plump, but her loose blouse and beautiful jewellery gave her a dignity that stirred all Sango's feelings for a home. She stood for a moment by the large velvet curtains, then came in and shook Sango's hand, warmly appraising him. At that moment all Sango's past despondency vanished and was replaced with a new desire: to be one of this proud family.

'So *you* are Amusa Sango! Welcome, thrice welcome!'

But if Sango had hoped to have Beatrice the Second to himself – even for two minutes – he was soon disillusioned. She came in a few moments before the meal was served: a younger edition of her mother – slighter of build, therefore looking taller. Less gold and jewellery about her throat and bare arms, and a haircut like a boy's. She smiled very sweetly when her eyes met Sango's but often he caught her in a brown study.

She sat on her father's right, while Sango sat on her mother's right and felt honoured but tantalized. They had *jolof* rice and smoked antelope. Beatrice's father was one of the few men in the city who believed in bush meat. He criticized the offerings of the butchers' stalls as 'tough and stringy'.

'How do you expect meat to taste good when the cattle walk eight hundred or more miles to the slaughter-house? I have my own hunter!'

He talked about his youth and the days when the Portuguese and the Brazilians, the French and the Dutch, the British and the Germans were fighting for trade supremacy on the West Coast of Africa.

'I was a small boy then, and never dreamed of marrying my wife. Now, after fifty-odd years of British rule, we hear talk of self-government.'

He believed in the Realization Party, though people accused it of belonging to the 'upper classes'. And why not? Was he himself not of the upper classes? When, after a chieftaincy battle, he had fled across the mangrove swamps of the Gulf of Guinea to this city – all the way from Dahomey – had he not himself been a chief over thousands?

'I believe in the past,' the old man said, when the meal was over. 'It is when you know the past that you can appreciate the present. We need something like the Realization Party to preserve our kingship, our music, art and religion!'

'You have come with your old talk, Papa Beatrice! The young man wants to talk to Beatrice. Let us leave them to play music and talk in their own way.'

Sango's ears stood open expectantly.

'Yes, Mama Beatrice, that is right. But this is a thinking young man – that is why I talk in this manner. Is that not so, Mr Sango? Are you tired of my company?'

'No, no, no! Not in the least. I enjoy listening to our history from a man who has lived through it!'

'Fine!' He smiled triumphantly and tapped his snuff-box. 'In my days when a man went to marry a woman it was a family affair. For instance, this medical student who is engaged to Beatrice. I know his father and mother. They are people who matter. They can offer my daughter security. I am proud to link my name with theirs, and they in turn are flattered. People talk loosely of love! Lovers cannot exist in a vacuum but in a society. This society demands certain things of them . . .'

He went on, harping on his point till Sango became suspicious. This old man was trying to discourage him; but at the end of the evening, he was more resolved than ever to win her, obstacles notwithstanding.

When he got home he wrote to his mother about Beatrice. Then he took the first step towards reinstating himself in a job. He wrote to various government departments – the last thing he had vowed to do in his life. It was all a farce, and when later on the replies came to say there were no vacancies he was not surprised or disappointed. Now he was well and truly up against the city which attracted all types. He had been very smug in his job as crime reporter for the *West African Sensation*.

At night he stood in for other people in their own bands. His motto had become money, money, money. This was the way the people of the city realized themselves. Money. He saw the treachery, intrigue, and show of power involved. Sometimes he earned twenty shillings a night for blowing his trumpet within smelling distance of a wet and stinking drain. He discovered the haunts of the sailors whose ships had anchored off the lagoon for a mere five days.

In these dens the girls were slick with too much of every-thing: too much lipstick, so that their lips were either caked or too invitingly moist: too much hips, too much of their thighs showing beneath their unfashionable skirts, too much breast bursting the super-tight blouses.

'But I have to stick it,' Sango murmured, and tightened his mind against the sordidness of his surroundings. 'Beatrice the Second must never know my humiliation.'

One evening, in the heat of jiving and jostling a white man slipped in. He was by no means the only white man there for most of the sailors were white, but this stranger had the rare look of a gentleman and was decidedly out of place. Where everyone had on a loud coat-type shirt outside pole-clinging trousers and pin-point shoes, he came in evening dress with the Savile Row cut, and worn in that way peculiar to the well-bred Englishman away from home. He certainly could not be expected to 'dig' the others.

With due respect they gave him a seat in an isolated corner, and as he sat down, Sango saw his face: 'Grunnings!'

A steward came towards him and took his order. When he returned with the drinks and cigarettes, Grunnings pointed at the dance floor. The steward nodded; then went over to a tall girl in red jeans and scarlet lipstick that contrasted rudely with her chocolate skin. He whispered in her ear. Some moments later, she was sitting opposite Grunnings and smoking his cigarettes.

She was such a contrast to the elegant Beatrice the First that Sango could not disguise his shock. What had become of Grunnings's taste? Had his desire for a bed-partner driven him to the lowest sex-market?

When Grunnings left, Sango learnt that he had come here in search of Beatrice the First. The girl in the red jeans said: 'Why he come ask me? I be sister of the girl? Me don' know where she stay!'

Sango was touched. Grunnings had actually loved Beatrice the First – more than she knew or cared. His playing acquired a plaintive note, and before dawn he was too exhausted to do more than drag himself into bed. Over and over again, he thanked his stars that in this city he had a friend like First Trumpet. But for him, life as it now was would have been unbearable.

15

The railway platform was crowded with Muslims in robes
and turbans who had come to welcome a pilgrim from Mecca.
Sango strolled among them, but soon found a remote seat
and brought out the telegram. He read it again:

A RELAPSE: COMING TO CITY FOR OPERATION.

It was from his mother and he was afraid this time. When
the train arrived, Sango was admitted into the special com-
partment where she lay. Blue-grey light filtered into the air-
conditioned cell, and as the door shut behind him the yelling,
chattering and sobbing from the platform was switched out
with a click.

'My son,' she murmured.

She was very thin, but her skin was well preserved. In her
face Sango could see a gentle rebuke in the helpless expression
that suffering had given it. He was stimulated tenderly. He
realized suddenly the deep bond that existed between him
and her; and through her the customs that were of the older
generation – like his having to marry Elina. All this flashed
through his mind in one revealing moment as he gazed calmly
on her face.

'You are well and strong?'

'Yes, mother.'

It was all that concerned her. So long as he was well and
strong, there was hope. He felt that hope surged through him.
His troubles paled before her presence.

'Elina and her mother came with me. Have you seen them?
They are in the third class.'

This was awkward. It meant that his mother was tired of talk and had brought the girl with her to make sure that her son was now safely out of danger from the women of the city.

The stretcher-bearers did not leave them much longer. With care they took her out of the carriage and into the ambulance that waited outside the station. Sango caught a bus to the General Hospital to make sure how she was looked after and how things were fixed for the next few days. A nurse told him he could not go in, but he was satisfied that she was in C.6 and that her bed was screened away from curious eyes.

In the corridor he bumped into a fair-skinned girl chaperoned by an elderly woman.

'I'm Elina!'

'You!' She had grown from the scraggy, timid girl he had seen in the Eastern Greens into a kind of 'poster' girl. No one advertising the Girl Guide Movement or the Women's this or that service could afford to overlook her. She had an air of calm response and confidence that put one at ease.

Sango explained how it was that he could not take them to his home. They were not used to hotels and restaurants either, and were frightened of the idea of going to eat and talk in public. Finally Sango suggested a seat by the lagoon; they could at least watch the canoes and the ocean liners moving about. At least for people who had been inland all the time the sea had its fascination.

They sat long on those benches talking, and eventually someone mentioned the dreaded word 'marriage'. Sango looked up sharply and said he was not planning to marry for the next ten years. There was something about Elina which made him feel she just did not 'belong'.

'Elina can go into the convent,' Sango said. 'The convent in this city is good enough and she'll learn quite a bit.'

She shook her head. 'Elina is going nowhere. She'll look after me and that's enough. I do not intend to let her out of my sight *in this city*!'

'I could stay here for ever watching the lagoon!' Elina said, and her mother looked at ango triumphantly. 'Didn't I tell you?' her eyes seemed to say. 'This city is no good for a girl so young – unless, of course, she has a husband!'

He saw them home. They had arranged to stay with a relation till Sango's mother got well, and they would go back to the Eastern Greens. Their relation turned out to be a clerk in the Survey Department. With a wife and child he occupied two spacious rooms with a kitchen at the back. The quarters were clean and well planned for clerks in the civil service, but the occupants complained of being remote from the centre of things.

When Sango left them he went immediately to search for Beatrice the Second.

The junction of Jide and Molomo Streets was perhaps the most central spot in the whole city. Someone had once said that if you remained long enough in the barber's shop, you were bound to see the people who mattered in the city. On this morning, Sango sat down and revolved the chair so that he had eyes on the street. It was a dull morning, threatening, but never seeming to rain. The sun was invisible, but the air was cool and crisp without being sticky.

In the distance, Sango saw a lorry bearing the colourful letters:

TRAVEL TO GOLD COAST OVERLAND

He sat up. It was Kofi. He ran into the street, waving. The lorry slid clumsily to the left side of the road and stopped. Kofi came down.

'Sango, is that you?'

'What's wrong, Kofi? Where's Beatrice? Why are your eyes so red?'

He took out a handkerchief and pressed to his eyes. Sango was embarrassed. The poor man was weeping.

'Dead . . . she died last week.' He coughed and blew. 'And what pains me most . . . she was buried as a pauper. No one to claim her. I – I —' He could say no more.

They crossed the street to the barber's shop. Kofi found a seat. He was breathing deeply as though trying to compose his feelings.

'I have often asked, why do girls leave their happy homes and come here on their own? No brothers, no knowledge of anything, no hope . . . They just come to the city, hoping that some man will pick them up and make them into something. Not just one man. You can't find him at the right time. But *many men*. And some disease, something incurable picks them up. You see them dressed, and they are just shells. Hollow and sick . . .' He did not lift his head as he talked.

'But she was happy with you, Kofi! When I saw you on that day, you were just returning from the Gold Coast —'

'That's what you saw. We looked happy. You did not under-stand what was underneath. How could you? The girl was finished, man.' He looked up and Sango could not bear to see his red eyes. 'Finished, I say. I was trying to help her back. She was finished, I tell you; and I was the last man, and too late. The helping hand had come too late. Look, man to man, I have my own wife at home on the Gold Coast, and I rent a house here. And these your girls, I can't resist them! They're too beautiful. And I can't bring my own wife here. Of course she does not know about Beatrice, how can she? But now I must stop all that nonsense; it is not sweet when you lose a woman you love. You know, I did not know I could love her. It was a business arrangement, pure and simple.'

He stared into the street. A woman carrying oranges swung her hips and made eyes. She had balanced the oranges pre-cariously and was peeling one. Kofi looked at her, then turned to Sango.

'Tell me, why did she come to this city at all? Why did I have to know her?'

'I'll tell you why she came, Kofi. She was not content with poverty. Remember, not many people like to remain where fate has placed them. I have known the home of Beatrice.

I can tell you. And if you have been there yourself, you would not condemn her actions. She was running away from it.'

Kofi shook his head slowly, no less than a hundred times. The truth was sinking in. 'But she threw her life away. The city eats many an innocent life like hers every year. It is a waste of our youth! It must stop.'

Sango laughed. 'Secret societies eat a lot more. But what do the People of the City care? Nothing whatever. They have created the flitter and they are content to live in it. Yes, yes. The irony of Fate. The strange turns of justice . . .'

Kofi was weeping again. If he continued in this manner he would never be able to see the road for tears. He sat with Sango and they talked and talked and still he wanted to know why Beatrice had come to the city. He would never be satisfied with any answer because he was not really seeking an answer, only venting his bitterness at the loss.

When Sango accompanied him across the street he was talking to himself like a man distracted. It was something very sad to see.

She rose when he entered; tied the cloth more firmly about her hips, swelling out her breasts as she did so. She walked vainly to the table, poured herself a glass of water. There was a time when Sango would have thought the dimples at the back of her knees nice and soft, but not now. When she turned and faced him he recognized her for what she was – the dark temptress who was such a threat to his happiness, especially now that his mother was here.

'What are you doing here, Aina?'

'No need to shout, Sango. I've come to rest. I'm short of money, so I came.'

'Short of money? Is this the bank? And did I not give you some money a short time ago?'

'Five pounds will not last for ever. I tried to manage it, but I have a lot of things to buy, to prepare myself for the coming baby —'

'Quickly now! I don't want you here again!'

Nothing showed the condition she claimed to be in; in fact, if anything, she had grown more attractive. Sango admitted this grudgingly and at the same time decided what he must do. It must have shown in his eyes.

'Amusa, why do you look at me so? You frighten me with your eyes! Oh, let me go before you kill me!'

'Quickly!

'I beg you – let me tie my wrapper properly before entering the street.' She was at the door.

'Aina, come back! You silly fool.'

He moved quickly and seized her garment from the rear. He heard it wrench. All the pent-up madness snapped in his brain and he slapped her face till his hands hurt.

'Let me go!' she cried.

In her panic she was clawing and biting noisily, and as she wrenched herself free, Sango saw with alarm how she held her sides in pain. Her knees buckled . . . she collapsed and fell. Incredible! He had not hurt her, surely! A thousand fears raced through his brain. He was in real panic. Suppose she died in this room?

When First Trumpet returned, Aina was still in a coma, and there was much water on the floor of the room. All the savagery had now died out of Sango and he wondered how she had provoked him into such brutality.

'What have you done?' First Trumpet moaned in dismay. 'Now we're both in the soup.'

'My nerves! I must have lost my head.'

'I know a private doctor,' said First Trumpet. 'I'm going to fetch some help.'

Sango heard him later in the street, hailing a taxi.

He could not decide whether to be pleased or sorry, for Aina was having a miscarriage. That she was in great pain he knew and did not like to contemplate the degree of her suffering. At the same time he did not completely forget the unsatisfied desire to avenge the injustice he had suffered at her hands. He was glad she might live, glad she had not involved him in a sensational accident.

He prayed that Aina would live. If she did, he vowed once and for all to end this evil relationship with the temptress who always awakened the meanest traits in him. Ultimately everything would depend on Aina's not passing away during this misfortune, because everything could easily be traced back to that quarrel. The lawyers (who had not been present) would describe in detail how Sango – 'all six feet of him, and he's not a weakling either' – had brutally assaulted this girl of delicate and feeble build . . . No! A disheartening picture which he did not like to pursue. On the other hand, if she lived, her mother might want to claim damages. She was that kind of shrewd woman who pressed her rights to the very end.

At visiting time he called at the shady little hospital accompanied by Beatrice the Second. They waited for a moment in the sitting-room overlooking a congested drain.

'You've come to see Aina,' said a nurse, opening the door. 'Come in – but only for a few minutes. The patient must not be disturbed. Please do not wake her. I believe she's asleep. Follow me.'

She closed the door behind them. There was only one chair in the room. Beatrice sat on it. The air was close and antiseptic. There was so much white linen around that Aina looked like a saint. She was very pale.

'Look,' said Beatrice. 'She's stirring. We promised —'

Aina's eyes flickered open. 'Sango, my love. Are you here? Hold my hand.'

Beatrice looked awkwardly at them both. 'Go on, Sango. Hold her hand.'

'What have you brought me?' Aina said, seizing Sango's extended hand.

'Fruits,' said Beatrice. She raised the basket for Aina to see.

'Sango, who is this girl? Your new wife? The one you went to marry in the Eastern Greens?'

'We're not married – yet!'

'You can marry now. What are you waiting for? You see, Amusa, we girls love you so much. I don't know why. You do not treat us so well, but we love you. I wanted you to marry me. And this girl, it is in her eyes.'

Sango found the room particularly hot at that moment. He did not know where to turn his gaze. 'You're weak, Aina. Don't worry yourself too much —'

Aina began to sob. 'The women go for you, and you only hurt them as you hurt me . . .' She was sobbing loudly now.

The nurse came in. 'You must leave now.' She was angry. 'Didn't you promise not to wake her? Next time —'

On the street, Beatrice held Sango's hand. 'You know something: what this girl said is true. The girls go for you. I am very worried myself. Recently, I have been feeling very lonely when you're not with me. I can't concentrate. I do things I have never done before – like telling lies to my father so that they don't know I've come to see you . . .'

Sango was beside himself with joy. There was hope for him, then! He did not want to dwell on it because he did not see how Beatrice could ever be his – with all that family matchmaking her father had talked about.

'Have courage, Amusa. All will be well for you – and for me!'

'Good night, dear B.'

He stood on the street corner until she climbed the steps of her father's house.

Sango was told by a nurse in a white mask and rubber gloves that visitors were not allowed anywhere near the theatre. Everything would be all right, she said, and he need not worry.

He walked in the hospital garden among the mango trees. If only he could go in there and see his mother. No. That would not do. It would make Soye too self-conscious. Soye had said. 'I'll do my best for you,' and that was good enough. Soye was a brilliant surgeon, one of the few select Africans with an F.R.C.S. to his name. Still, he was no god. He could still be handicapped by lack of facilities.

He went back to the waiting-room. There was a girl in a pale blue frock sitting at the other end of the bench. It was no time to notice girls, but Sango's heart began to race much faster. And when the girl turned her face, he was sure.

'Beatrice! Beatrice the Second!'

'Oh, Amusa! How's your mother?'

He could not believe his eyes. Beatrice the Second had a sad tale to tell. Her fiancé, around whom she had built all her plans, had been flown back home from England. His condition was critical. He had been found in a gas-filled chamber at the hostel soon after the results of his examination had been announced. Of course he had always been of a brooding temperament, taking things far too seriously. Beatrice told how his greatest ambition had always been to be a doctor and how he had worked far too hard with far too little success. Beatrice was too distressed to speak about her problems in full. Nor did Sango question her too closely. It was enough to know that they were partners in sorrow. A nurse called Beatrice into one of the wards.

Hours later, it seemed, Dr Soye came out. One glance at his face and Sango knew the worst. The doctor pressed his hand.

'Very sorry; she was getting so well before the relapse.'

Relapse . . . relapse . . . the ugly word again. He could not make out exactly what was happening in the tottering world around him. Everybody was having a relapse. The nurse in spotless white was smilingly telling him how sorry she was. Beatrice was holding his hand, leaning close to him.

'Had you come when you got the message?' said the nurse.

'What message? This is just a routine visit. Nobody told me anything.'

'Your mother wanted to see you,' said the nurse. 'Of course, that was shortly after the woman left her bedside.'

'I know of no woman. Can you describe her?'

The world began to reel round in circles. Sango put the pieces together as she spoke and the pieces made only one picture: Aina's mother. The blackmailing woman of the tempting daughter. God alone knew what she had told the poor woman to bring about the relapse that killed her.

Hand in hand, he and Beatrice walked down the corridor. 'Who was the woman, I mean the visitor?'

'Later on, Beatrice. Later on.' Before they parted he said, 'I'm going to be busy with arrangements. Can you come to the funeral? Tomorrow at four.'

He saw the tears in her eyes and did not wait for an answer.

Sango had no pretext on which to enter Twenty Molomo Street. Not now, after all that had happened. All he could do in his off moments was to go there and sit in the barber's shop. It was always restful and anyone who sat there saw the city unroll before his eyes, a cinema show that never ended, that no producer could ever capture – the very soul of man.

It was his old boy Sam who told him that Lajide had drunk himself to death. 'Yes sah! He die wonderful death. Everybody wonder how he die . . . they don' know what ah know. The man drink too much! Gin – every time. O.H.M.S. – illicit gin, the one they make in the bus.'

Lajide's end had come suddenly. Like this – he got up in the morning, put on some clothes. He was to go to court that morning. Then he complained that he felt queer. He stretched himself on the bed, fell into a coma and was taken to hospital. There he passed peacefully away without ever recovering consciousness.

The thought of death terrified him. I must see Aina tonight at *that* address. The words hammered in his brain. Tonight, at that address. Who knows – perhaps she's dead! There's too much death now among the people of the city. It is as if they have all played at the big cinema show and are coming to its conclusion. After seeing Aina, if she's still alive, I must play at *that* wretched Club. They'll now pay only seventeen and six a night. Still, I must recover my funeral expenses.

Sam was telling him about a brother of Lajide's – a farmer who had a limp and rode a bicycle. A bicycle – when Lajide changed cars once a year. The whole compound was locked and bolted and all the wives had gone home to their mothers. With a sly wink Sam explained how the wives had refused to be taken over by the limping brother.

'Ha, ha! He take all his brother's things; but he no fit to take the wives!'

As they spoke a man riding a bicycle dismounted and began to limp towards the entrance.

'Tha's him, sah. Tha's Lajide's brother.'

Not long after that, a car which looked like Zamil's drew up. A Lebanese in dark glasses strode towards Number Twenty, brought out a bundle of keys and let himself in, followed by Lajide's brother.

'Them say he done sell him brother house,' Sam whispered. All the people in the street seemed to have gathered, and though it was no business of theirs they were whispering and pointing and watching every move.

Sango would always love Molomo Street. Nothing could ever be secret here, and it made nonsense of taking life too seriously. They were all – each and every one of them – members of one family, and what concerned one concerned all the others.

16

Because Beatrice the Second had lost her fiancé, because she had tried once – unsuccessfully – to run away from home, because her mother thought the girl was old enough at twenty-two to marry whom she chose and her father could not bear the thought of his illustrious name soiled by a scandal, because the name 'Amusa Sango' had rung in the ears of father and mother every minute for the last six months (banned though it had been), because of all this and much more, it was decided that the wedding should take place as quietly as possible.

Sango did not waste much time. The old man's whims were unpredictable and he could withdraw his consent at any moment. Beatrice had again affirmed her desire that her life be Sango's with no further delay.

They took a special licence at Sant Amko's magistrate's court, and the reception was held at Jogun Lane, where Beatrice's parents lived.

Sango's old friends came in their remaining force: the barber, limping as usual, casting curious eyes at Aina and her mother. 'Ah-ah! But Mr Sango,' he whispered in an aside. 'Why you don' marry Aina? The gal like you too much. Why you don' marry her?'

Sango merely smiled. If only the barber knew the depth and complications of their relationships! If only he knew what Sango had escaped by that fleeting love affair begun under the shadows of Molomo Street!

But God must be praised for bringing back Aina's life.

The private doctor had done his bit, of course, and had got his pay. But it had been precarious. That borderline between life and death: Aina had hovered on it threateningly for many a soul-searing night. If she had crossed, who would have believed that he never meant to harm her in the first place? Or that the child she had, belonged to another man? Who – in this wide city?

He looked at her. She was smiling. Still pale, her coming here showed that she was a sport, a good loser. Perhaps life had taught her that: perhaps she still hoped . . . The gramophone was playing and those who felt happier than Sango were dancing and drinking beer.

These did not include the father of Beatrice, who sat like a statue, apparently moaning his loss. Now and again he eyed Sango challengingly – a challenge Sango vowed in his young heart to accept in the smallest detail. It was not only those who were born into high society who became somebody. Sure, they began with a bigger advantage, but that did not mean they ended with their breasts against the winning tape.

'I'll show him. Or rather – we'll show him!'

And he looked at the face of Beatrice and from it drew all the courage he desired. At his request she had put on a cool blue frock – simple, without frills. He knew her preference for native wear which added a little more fullness to her figure and with it a little more dignity.

Elina and her mother must be far away now. They had caught the first train to the Eastern Greens and would probably almost be there. Sango wondered why he thought of them at this moment. And he wondered too, what it would have been like to see Elina sitting at a sewing-machine in that room with the lace curtains, idly making a dress while around her sat her friends, sipping lime-juice and eating chicken, a mixture of bashfulness, joy and sorrow.

'Amusa! Amusa!' It was Beatrice.

On hearing the happiness in her voice, everyone seemed to feel her longing for the man she loved. And they began to leave.

In the corridor, Sango found himself face to face with Aina's mother.

'Sango, your mother was a wonderful woman. She loved you so much! Do you know she died of *happiness*? When she heard you were to be a father, she was so glad. She said, "Thank God, he is becoming something at last." So she said, and I swear to you I am speaking the truth. She told me to fetch you at once, that she might see you. She was very glad! But I didn't know where to find you then. You must forgive me, Sango,' she said and pressed the edge of her cloth to her eyes. 'You see, I went there to spoil your name before your mother. Because of Aina. But your mother was above it all!'

Sango saw her to the door. Aina stood there, crestfallen. There were genuine tears in her eyes and a hint of rebuke. She had broken down at last. Sango looked at her, embarrassed.

'Travel to Gold Coast, Overland!'

'Kofi! Hello, Kofi. You just coming when everybody is leaving!'

'Travel to Gold Coast Overland,' said the boisterous man. 'Come with me, and bring your bride.'

'Who told you, Kofi?' said Sango.

'There's no secret in this city. You took a special licence, and you tried to hide yourself. You think no one will know . . . Listen, Amusa. I'm all right now. I've recovered from the loss of my Nigerian girl friend. I'm not so sad as last time when we met. It was horrible then.'

Sango looked at Beatrice and smiled. 'Our secret is out, B!'

'Let's go to the Gold Coast. I have always wanted to go there.' There was a plea in Beatrice's voice.

'Yes. We want a new life, new opportunities . . . We want to live there for some time – but only for some time! We have our homeland here and must come back when we can answer your father's challenge! When we have *done* something, *become* something!'

'Travel to Gold Coast Overland! By Kofi Transport! It is

safe, sure and slow.' Kofi by now had a glass of beer in his hand and was behaving as though the contents had taken effect. 'But it will get you there – in peace.'

'Not in pieces,' Beatrice and Sango laughed together.

Beatrice had slipped her hand under Sango's arm. 'Amusa, let's snatch happiness from life *now* – now, when we're both young and need each other.' She was smiling and her eyes searched his face.

Yet contradicting that smile was the tiny pearl of a tear which he saw stealing down her cheek. He embraced her tenderly, murmuring into her hair.

'God bless you – and *us*!'

OTHER NEW YORK REVIEW CLASSICS

For a complete list of titles, visit www.nyrb.com or write to:
Catalog Requests, NYRB, 435 Hudson Street, New York, NY 10014